Wander & Roam

a novel by

A N N A   K Y S S

To Megan ~
I hope you enjoy!

Anna Kyss

Wander & Roam

a novel by

ANNA KYSS

Prologue

When my cell phone rings, I ignore it and pull the covers over my head. If Robbie were still around, I would jump to answer my phone. Now, I prefer to burrow under my comforter and block everyone out.

The ding of a voicemail competes against the pounding at my door. I can't imagine who would be bothering me. My friends haven't come around in weeks.

"Abby, I know you're inside," Nicole, the residence advisor for our floor, calls. "We need to talk."

Great, what does she want? It can't be good news.

I stumble out of bed and open the door. Nicole scrutinizes me from head to toe. Her gaze lingers on my mussed hair and wrinkled pajamas before shifting to the growing pile of soiled clothes on the floor.

"How long has it been since you left your room?" she asks.

I sigh. "Why does it matter?"

"You haven't even collected your mail." She deposits a pile of letters and pamphlets into my hands. After I set them down, she hands me an official-looking envelope. "This one must be opened immediately. Dean's orders."

The Dean. Oh no. I thought if I hid away up here, I could escape everyone's notice, but that theory didn't work. I slowly tear open the envelope.

Notice of Academic Dismissal. The large, bolded words are impossible to ignore. I quickly scan the letter. *Poor attendance. Missing assignments in all classes. Unexcused absences during mid-*

term testing. Low grade point average.

I can't think of grades and assignments when Robbie's gone. Most days, I don't want to function without him.

The final line catches my attention. *Must vacate premises within the month.* "Nicole, what does this mean?"

She presses her lips together before glancing around my messy room. "You've been kicked out."

I breathe in once, twice, three times, before asking, "Isn't there any kind of appeal? I can't move home."

Nicole holds out her hands, exasperated. "If you had responded to the first three letters that were sent, you could have appealed. It's too late, Abby."

Too late. This isn't the first time I've heard those two words. They, like nearly everything else, remind me of Robbie.

She heads out the door. "I'm sorry to be the bearer of bad news. Good luck finding new housing."

I lock the door and crumple to the floor. *How am I possibly going to explain this to my parents?* My father's already been hounding me for weeks. When I check the missed call, it lists Home. Reluctantly, I listen to the message.

"Abigail, it's your father. Since you never seem to pick up your phone anymore, I'll have to communicate my concerns via voicemail. I'm still waiting for you to forward your midterm grades to me. I can't emphasize the importance of keeping your GPA as high as possible this year. Graduate schools consider all four years and if you slip up, well… we've had this conversation before. Call your mother. She misses hearing your voice. I hope this lack of communication is due to diligent studying, rather than stewing about that boy."

That boy. I delete the rest of his message and throw down my phone. *How could he possibly refer to Robbie as "that boy?"* After everything I've been through.

My tidy desk stands out against the backdrop of dirty laundry, old food, and trash. Its wooden surface contains only four things: notebook paper, a supply of pens, and two neat stacks of purple envelopes.

I settle at the desk, take out a fresh piece of paper, and place my pen to the page.

Dear Robbie, I need you more than ever.

For the next fifteen minutes, I pour out my agitation, worries, and fears on the page. With each new sentence, my body calms. When I've leaked every last drop of emotion onto the paper, I seal it into one of the purple envelopes. I kiss the envelope and place it atop the stack of other sealed ones. Even if I never send them, the orderly purple pile brings me comfort.

I can't return home. I would never survive the lectures and the shaming. I'm barely enduring already.

I slide back into bed but send the pile of mail soaring across my comforter. A pamphlet lands near my pillow, and the letters catch my eye. WWOOF.

Worldwide Opportunities on Organic Farms. The pamphlet describes how the organization is recruiting volunteers for small, organic farms around the world. Lodging and meals are complimentary. More importantly, they have immediate openings.

Perfect.

After doing some research online, I settle on the most remote farm I can find. Australia. I have a passport, so that's not an issue. When I check my spending account balance, it has barely moved this semester, not surprising since I never go out. One of the benefits of self-isolation, I suppose. I have enough money for a round-trip ticket and a little extra for spending expenses.

Maybe flying halfway round the world is exactly what I need. I can isolate to my heart's desire, and no one will ask me about my past. If I run far enough, maybe I can outdistance the things that haunt me.

Chapter
1

As I stand at the motorboat's bow, briny water covers me in a light mist. Salty droplets crystallize on my nose and cheeks in the hot summer sun. Even my denim shorts and sunshine yellow tank don't take away the incongruity of summer in December. I should be bundled up in sweaters, a scarf, and mittens, rather than letting my body soak in the delicious warmth. December is the time to gather with family, build snowmen with my herd of nieces and nephews, cozy under a blanket for a movie with...

Which is exactly why I'm here and not back home in Ohio; too many memories. I can't bear to watch my family laugh and love when my happiness is gone. December is the month of memories, and all I want is to escape the destruction of mine.

The blurred shore comes into focus, and I study each detail. A single trail leads from the dock up the wooded hillside. Lush vegetation, rather than houses or buildings, covers the land, which is exactly how I want it. Isolation sounds lovely.

Then I spot a guy resting upon the dock. His bronzed skin stands out from the pale winter flesh I just left behind.

Looking at the muscles swelling beneath that golden skin, I try to guess his age. He appears more mature than the boys in my dorm do, but there's something youthful about him, too. Maybe it's the way he sits along the edge of the dock, a smile on his face and his feet in the water.

His bare feet make little ripples as they splash around in the bay. His rolled-up jeans dip daringly close to the water but remain dry. He raises one foot out of the water, points it in my direction, and waves.

I lift my gaze past his jeans, past his bare chest, to his face. His smile widens and he waves again, using his hand this time. I slide to the bottom of the boat then slump against the side so it hides my entire body. I cannot believe he caught me staring—no, ogling, him.

What's even harder to believe is that I *was* looking, and I actually enjoyed what I saw. The guilt serves as a cool pail of water dumped over my flaming cheeks. It damps the fires of embarrassment.

More waves threaten to come unless I find my notebook. Frantically, I search my backpack for it. My trusty pen is woven in the metal looping. I place it against the fresh page and sigh as the words pour out:

I never imagined I would be here, halfway across the world, without you. It doesn't feel fair I have the freedom to explore, while you are...
Why couldn't we travel through Australia hand-in-hand? Of course, if we could be together, I wouldn't be here to begin with. Funny thing I'm learning, though. No matter how far you run, you can't outdistance your problems.
I miss you, Robbie.
Abby

I carefully tear out my letter before folding it and placing it into a small purple envelope. As the envelope joins the others, my heart slows, my muscles calm, and my mind relaxes. Finally in control, I slip on my backpack and stand up, only to find myself staring in the eyes of Mr. Bronze.

"You must be the new volunteer." He doesn't speak with any of the exotic Australian dialects I was expecting.

"You're American?" I carefully make my way off the boat and onto the wooden dock.

A dimple appears as he smiles. "Most people call me Sage, but I'll go by 'American' if you want."

I peg him as a Midwesterner, just like me. "I'm Abby."

Sage lifts my big suitcase out of the water taxi. "Do you have all your things?"

"It's just the suitcase and backpack."

He rests the suitcase on the grass then returns to the water taxi. "Susan wanted me to thank you for giving our new volunteer a ride. We'll see you next Tuesday?"

The driver nods before revving away.

Tiny waves lap along the shore. After finding a sunny spot, I plop to the ground and stare out over the water. While this isn't an ocean, the bay is one of the largest bodies of water I've ever seen. Well, except for Lake Erie, but the grossness factor of that pollution-ridden lake rules it out.

Sage sits next to me on the grass. "How did you find your way to such a remote Australian farm?"

His question reminds me why I started avoiding my friends and teachers at the university. People ask too many darn questions.

My silence doesn't stop him. He asks, "Are you exploring, growing, or running?"

I stare at him. *How has he figured me out so quickly?*

"Interesting, I wouldn't have pegged you for a runner. The big question is what are you running from?" His eyes—brown, speckled with gold—meet mine.

"I don't talk about my past." I need to send our talk in a different direction quickly. I haven't had a real conversation in so long, I'm rusty and out of practice. After a long pause, I decide to ask about the one thing we probably have in common, volunteering on this farm. "How did you end up WWOOFing?"

"I'm an explorer and a grower. The timing seemed right to live in a different country, learn how to farm, and practice."

"Practice?" Practice what? My mind flutters from sports

activities to musical instruments, but none seems to fit.

"I could talk for hours about practicing." Sage shakes his longish curls, also brown streaked with gold. "I don't want to bore you on your first day, though."

"You mentioned Susan. How do you like working at her farm?" I have no idea what to expect while farming. Despite the number of farms in the Midwest, most of us, me included, live in the suburbs.

"I arrived two weeks ago. And I love every moment of farming."

"So are you hoping to leave a better-rounded, worldlier person? Or will this just look good on some job application or graduate school resume?" I can't believe how long we've been talking. This may be the longest conversation I've had in the past six months.

Sage takes a turn at the silent game. He stares down at the ground for a long moment before muttering, "I don't want to talk about my future."

I'm all too familiar with his reaction. We could make a good team. Me running from my past and him avoiding his future.

"Let's make a deal. I promise to not ask about your past, if you don't talk about my future."

"What's left?" I imagine an entire month of no conversations. While I'm not super outgoing, zero talking might be a bit extreme.

"The 'now.' We live in the 'now.'" He watches me until I nod my approval.

Raising my water bottle, I toast, "To the present."

"To the present," he toasts back with a water bottle of his own.

Chapter 2

"Oh good, you arrived safely." The petite woman wears the biggest sunhat I have ever seen. Her black hair is twisted into two thick braids hanging past her waistline. "I'm Susan, your host."

"Abby." I hold out my hand. When she turns to greet me, I spot the baby tied to her back.

"And this cute little guy is Zachary." Sage tickles one of the baby's bare feet, and Zachary giggles in response.

The land flattens into a grassy plateau with trails leading up, down, and to the sides. In the distance, I spot a small house. Susan's home, probably. The wild vegetation tames into cultivated garden beds to my far right.

"You must be exhausted after your trip. I'll show you to your room." Susan leads me to the uppermost trail. "You brought a *suitcase*?"

I grab its handle. The wheels are battered from the mile-long, rock-strewn trail. "Yeah, I didn't pay close enough attention to that part of your email."

"Thankfully, I sent Sage down to collect you." Susan eyes the large suitcase.

'Thankfully' was the right word. Sage and I had taken turns pulling my monster of a bag up the rugged trail. As an Ohio girl, I'm used to the carefully sculpted and sometimes even paved trails forming the wilds of the suburbs, the metro parks. One Australian hike demonstrated just how manufactured nature was back home.

I glance down the steep slope leading back to the dock. The thick tree cover nearly blocks the view of the bay, with only brief glances of the blue water visible between the branches. Still exhausted from that climb, I'm not sure if I'm up for another.

"Ready?" Susan asks. "I can't wait to show off where you'll sleep."

"Sounds good." I can't wait to finally have some privacy after my nearly twenty-four hour journey.

"There's even a working bathroom up here. It took me the longest time to figure out how to manage that, but my contractor suggested connecting to our well system for water and installing a composting toilet." She smiles and adds. "It's all green."

From her look of pride, that must be a fact that many organic farm volunteers care about. I'm here for a completely different reason. Escape.

For the next few minutes, we hike in silence. I can't tug my giant suitcase, go uphill, and talk at the same time. Every few feet, I lower my bag to the ground and catch my breath. Finally, the trail levels off, and we're able to make quicker progress.

She steps onto an even smaller footpath. The narrow path winds its way through exotic-looking shrubs and unusual flowers. "The guest cottage sits right off this trail."

"Cottage" is definitely a euphemism. A wooden platform holds an enormous, round, tent-like structure. The wooden door stands out against the canvas material covering the sides. Small details, like the potted flowers upon the wooden deck, make it homey.

"I'm going to be living in a tent?" I slowly walk up the steps to the deck.

Susan laughs, and little Zachary mimics her peals. "Well, technically, it's a yurt."

How is that different from a tent? I bite back my retort, though, not wanting to be rude.

She opens the door. "No need for a key. One of the benefits of living in nowhere."

Sunlight streams through the plastic windows and the skylight, turning the hardwood floor golden. Two wooden futons sit on opposite sides of the room. Their vibrant orange slipcovers accentuate the yurt's golden theme. Neatly folded sheets and blankets rest on the corner of one, while the other's bedding is haphazardly thrown in a bunch.

"Men." Susan sighs. "I asked Sage to make the guest yurt presentable."

"Sage?" She couldn't possibly mean...

"Both volunteers share the guest cottage. Didn't I mention that?"

"Um..." Not a word. I would have remembered *that*. I made a terrible assumption, though, thinking free accommodations equaled private accommodations.

"No worries." She waves her hand in the messy futon's direction. "Sage is as easy-going as can be. He'll make a great bunkmate."

His personality hasn't even crossed my mind. My worries center on how one look at Sage already triggered a letter-writing episode. If a short glance drives me to grab my pen, I can't imagine what cohabitating will do. Probably lead to the world's most epic writer's cramp.

My purple envelopes aren't limitless, after all.

Twenty minutes later, a knock sounds at the yurt door, followed by Sage's voice. "Can I come in?"

"Sure." I reach for the doorknob just as Sage peeks his head through. For a moment, we're only a hand's reach from one another. I step back so quickly, I nearly trip over my bag.

He props the door open with his body and holds up a bag of food. "I brought lunch. Thought you might be hungry after your long trip."

"Thanks." I glance around the yurt, but the room is too small to hold a table.

He points in the opposite direction of the bay. "I wouldn't mind sharing my super-secret picnic spot with you."

I'm so afraid of spending time with him—no, with anybody. Growing close to others only leads to pain in the long run.

"If you're too tired, I can take a rain check." He starts to separate the food.

Isolation has its downfalls, though. It led to being booted from school after I abandoned my classes. It led to my flight across the world so I could avoid the questions and concern of friends and family. Even Down Under, I'm unable to truly escape.

"Wait." I wave away the food. "Being outside sounds nice after all those hours on the plane."

Sage smiles. If he looked cute when he was serious, he's even more adorable when he grins. "You won't regret this," he says.

I already do.

Sage backtracks down the hill then leads us along a winding path until we reach the orchards. We pass through rows of bushes, dotted with still-green blueberries and plump, pink raspberries. At the far end, a grove of trees is planted in neat, equidistant rows.

As we step into the trees, each row hangs thick with various fruits, some familiar and others unrecognizable. I gently stroke a low-growing peach before following Sage into a grassy patch in the middle of the orchard.

Sage sits on the grass then pats the spot next to him. "You might be in for a surprise," he whispers.

"Surprise?"

"You'll see." He continues to speak in a quiet voice. "Susan makes a hot breakfast and dinner each day, served in the covered dining area near her home, and she packs sack lunches for me— well, I guess that's us now."

"Oh?" I examine the food he hands me. A sandwich stuffed with vegetables between two thick slabs of bread, a juicy peach, and homemade-looking granola bars.

"Susan's been making all the meals vegetarian, on account of me, but she'd be happy to cook up some dead animal, if you prefer."

I bite into my sandwich. The vegetable-only concoction doesn't taste terrible, but some thick slices of turkey would only make it better. "I prefer."

"Ah, you're a carnie." Sage sits back and watches me chew. I try to swallow my mouthful gracefully, but end up gulping awkwardly.

"Have you always been vegetarian?" I ask.

"What an esoteric question." Sage leans closer. "My follow-up question would be, in what life? Currently, I'm about to meet my two-month anniversary of veganism. But I imagine some of my past selves rejected meat entirely."

I stare at him. His expression is one of complete and total sincerity. "Do you actually believe that nonsense?"

Before he can answer, a deer-sized animal hops into the clearing. That's right. Hops. Two powerful back legs send it bounding underneath one of the plum trees. "Loo—"

Sage presses his soft, warm finger to my lips. I alternate between focusing on the brown critter nibbling at the fallen fruit in the orchard and his closeness.

He lowers his mouth to my ear and whispers, "They startle easily."

They? I haven't recovered from the tingle of his warm breath before I spot them. Four more animals, identical to the first, linger along the perimeter of the orchard.

"Wallabies," I silently mouth.

He presses his mouth to my ear once more. "Most people would have guessed kangaroos."

While they resemble kangaroos, they're too small. If I were standing, they would rise only to my waist. Movement-wise, though, they hop around similarly to the kangaroo.

How cool. I never planned to see Australian wildlife on my trip. The pleasure of watching the animals and eating with Sage fades. Coming here was never for leisure or fun. *How can I enjoy myself without Robbie?*

I stand abruptly, sending the wallabies scattering in all directions. "Thanks for lunch. I'll see you later."

Ignoring Sage's quizzical stare, I head back to the yurt. I need to lose myself in the relief of pen, paper, and purple envelopes.

Chapter
3

I can barely keep my eyes open as the first bands of sunlight stream into our yurt. I tossed and turned most of the night, managing to fall asleep only a few hours ago. While I'd like to blame my insomnia on jetlag, if I'm honest, the time difference only figured in the smallest amount.

Sage, on the other hand...

I've never shared living space with a guy. Even Robbie. Despite all the countless hours I hung out with him, we never spent the entire night together. It would have been too awkward, since he still lived with his parents.

Throughout the night, I was drawn to Sage. The rustle of his sheets, the soft exhale and inhale of his breaths, his smell; fresh, with a hint of spice.

Now that it's morning, I beat myself up over my attraction. If I were stronger—more loyal—I wouldn't even notice how the beam of light shining through the window accentuates the bronze highlights of his tanned face. I wouldn't pay any attention to the broad expanse of his shoulders as he stretches his muscular arms and yawns.

Groaning in frustration over these thoughts—unwanted, unbidden, yet irritatingly relentless—I hide my face in my pillow.

"Morning," Sage says. "Sleep well?"

A bell tolling in the distance saves me from answering. Thankfully. I truly don't know how I could have responded to that question.

"Breakfast's served." Sage pulls his shoes on. "Susan always rings the bell to let us know when meals are on the table. Ready?"

Not really. I wish I could have remained hidden away in my dorm at Erie University, northwest Ohio's most lackluster university. I had been lucky enough to get one of the new dorms, a single with an en-suite bathroom. With my mini-fridge, microwave, and coffee maker, I could hermit away as much as I liked.

Until they figured out I wasn't attending class or turning in assignments. Getting kicked out sucked. Surprisingly, I didn't miss the learning or my major or any of that. I yearned for the solitude, though.

"Well? Are you ready?" Sage holds the door open.

"Go ahead. I'll meet you there." I take a few moments to collect myself before grabbing my toiletry bag and heading to the bathroom.

When I heard about the composting toilet and well-fed sink and shower, I was nervous, but the bathroom's nicer than I anticipated. A large, glass-walled shower sits in one corner, and it even has one of those rainfall showerheads. The toilet looks pretty normal, until you notice that it isn't water-filled like the ones back home. Like the yurt, Susan's made the bathroom homey with a large bowl of flower and fruit potpourri.

After freshening up, I head down to the picnic tables. The covered eating area is just a short walk from Susan's home. Sage's voice and Susan's responding laughter grow louder as I walk. Great. More conversation and interaction, when all I want is to hide away from everybody. It's as if the world is conspiring against my isolation.

"age will show you the drill," Susan explains as we finish the last bites of waffles and fresh fruit. "I ask for five hours of labor a day, but you can divide the time up however you'd like."

"Susan's *very* flexible. *A bloody brilliant hostess.*" He pronounces the last sentence with a terrible Australian accent.

She smiles and shakes her head. "Sage always takes a post-lunch break before finishing his last two hours. I know it's lonely in the gardens by yourself, so feel free to join him."

Lonely sounds lovely. "Actually—"

Sage blurts out, "I can't have people butting in on my practice time. How will I focus?"

We look at one another. My cheeks warm, and he stares down, looking absolutely chagrined.

He runs one hand through his shoulder-length hair. "I'm sorry for being so rude. My practice time's the one time of the day—the only time, actually—that I need to be sort-of selfish."

"I don't mind. Being alone in the gardens sounds pretty nice, actually." I glance at Sage again. "So, what exactly do you practice?"

Susan clears our plates. "I'll let you finish this conversation as you head to the gardens. And Abby, it's so nice to have you with us."

Zachary peeks his head out from behind her and makes some of his cute baby noises. I hadn't even noticed him throughout breakfast.

"Finally awake? We need to change your nappy." She removes her wrap, skillfully bringing him from her back to her arms. "Come on, sweetie. Let's get you dry."

"Ready? I'll show you the way to the gardens from here." Sage holds out his hand to help me up. I ignore it, standing myself. When I peek at him, I can't miss the disappointment that flashes across his face. He hides it as soon as he notices me looking. I'm doing it again, spreading my misery to all those around me. It's how I ended up friendless and alone at school. Pushing *everyone* away.

The last fight I had with my parents focused on this issue. My mother's reprimand echoes through my memories. *Your misery doesn't give you license to make everyone around you miserable.*

"Is this the first time you've done this?" I force myself to smile.

He glances back, probably surprised by the brightness in my tone. "Done what? WWOOFing or traveling across the world?"

I shrug. "Either one. They're both firsts for me."

"Yeah, I've never done either before. I wish—" His voice falters, and he looks away. "I wish I had done more during high school. They offered a foreign exchange program where you could live in Europe for the semester, but I was too busy hanging with my buddies."

"Well, you're what—only twenty?"

"Twenty-one," he says.

"There's plenty of time still to see the world." I gesture around the farm. "This could be your first trip of hundreds."

"Yeah, I guess." He doesn't meet my eyes. "The gardens are just up ahead."

Large, raised beds fill the front half of the gardens, while neatly cultivated rows line the back. When I finally enter, climbing, spreading, growing things of all kinds surround me. I spend the first fifteen minutes wandering around and exploring each bed.

Tall green plants spill out of their wire cages. Their pencil-thin stems brim with bright, red tomatoes. Fragrant plants, short and leafy, fill in the tomato bed. When I place my nose to one, the aromatic scent brings to mind pesto. Basil. I pass fragile-looking vines laden with green beans, squat spreading vines with bright yellow flowers, and thick, flowering broccoli.

Sage kneels to examine a mystery bed filled with plants with wide green leaves and red stems. I can't figure out what they could be. "What do you think?"

"Amazing. Why don't more people have gardens back home?" I spin around. "Seeing so much growth and life everywhere feels healing."

Sage stares at me intensely. "I know just what you mean."

"I think I'm going to like volunteering here." I can't remember the last time I've thought in terms of looking forward to something. For so long, I only had things to dread.

Sage spends the next hour teaching me about each of the plants. Most of the plants I know, but I don't always recognize them in their natural form. By the time he finishes his tour, I can identify many of the plants in the garden, although I still have no idea how to care for any of them. Finally, he leads me to a bed of wispy-topped plants. Carrots.

"Carrots are a root vegetable. When their orange tops begin to poke out, they're ready to harvest." He guides my hands to a bit of orange peeking out of the soil then hand-over-hand shows me how to dig the carrots up.

I can barely concentrate on his words. The warmth of his hands against mine steals my focus. The rough callus on his thumb brushes over the top of my fingers. When I glance at Sage, he stares at me intensely. I didn't even notice when he stopped talking.

I jerk my hands away. Our awkward silence fills the gardens.

After a moment, Sage clears his throat. "I usually take my break just about now. Could you finish harvesting the carrots? Once you've finished this row, bring the basket to Susan."

He walks out of the gardens, leaving me with an empty wicker basket and a mind full of worries. As I free each carrot, I can't help but think about what just happened. My body betrayed me. *How could I be so drawn to someone I just met?*

I came here to escape the memories that plague me, not to carve out new layers of guilt. If this across-the-world trip is going to help, I need to stay away from Sage.

Chapter 4

I set the basket of carrots on the floor of the yurt. I should have brought the produce directly to Susan, but I couldn't wait another minute to write to Robbie.

I'm so confused. My heart's telling me to stay loyal, but my body is not in agreement. Having Sage live so close is like setting a chocolate cake, dripping with caramel and fudge frosting, on the table, but never taking a bite.

When I finally put pen to paper, my head clears and my mind calms. These letters help me keep control when I'm at my worst. Before I left school, my advisor recommended finding a good therapist. Therapy has always had such a bad stigma in my family, though.

I can imagine my dad's response. *A Bentley should be mentally strong enough to deal with any challenge.* Not one of my siblings ever needed extra help or mental health support. The very fact that I'm in Australia shows I would rather hide all the way round the world than bear disappointing my father.

But my feelings pour out through my pen, and despite Robbie's absence, it feels like he's listening when I seal my thoughts into his purple envelopes.

I tuck the envelope with all the others and pick up the basket of carrots. I can't delay delivering them any longer.

As I hike to Susan's house, I try to think of a plan. If I can avoid Sage, the issue will resolve itself. There have to be enough tasks on this farm that we can work separately. The bigger problem is our living situation. If only we had our own yurts.

I walk up the steps to Susan's deck and knock at her open back door. "I brought the carrots. Where would you like them?"

"You can leave them next to the door," Susan calls. "If you can wait a few minutes, I'll be along soon."

Susan's place differs from the cookie-cutter houses back home. Rather than the identical aluminum siding that covers entire neighborhoods in the Midwest, her house has sides formed from rough-sawn wood. The deck and wrap-around porch feature a hand-carved railing.

Flowerbeds surround the house, with some of the blooms growing higher than the railing. The house blends in perfectly with the picturesque backdrop of farm and wilderness, its tin roof being only a slightly lighter shade of green than the surrounding vegetation.

"Lovely, isn't it?" Susan steps onto the deck. "My grandfather built the house himself. It was his wedding present for my mother."

"Did he give her the land as well?"

"No, Nana and Pop lived in the city. When my mother fell in love with a farmer, they wanted her to have a comfortable life out here." Susan runs her hand along the railing. "Mum told me that my grandfather spent every weekend for six straight months working on his gift."

What would it be like to have such a supportive father? He couldn't have been happy that his daughter was moving away from him, but he gave up six months of his life to help her settle. I can't even tell my dad that I flunked out of school. He would never understand.

He didn't understand about Robbie, after all.

"What an amazing gift. I bet your family will treasure it for generations."

Susan's smile disappears. "I hope so. I really hope so."

I help Susan carry the baskets of carrots into her kitchen. She rests them on the floor then returns to the deck. Susan sits on a hanging porch swing then pats the seat next to her. "How have your first few days gone?"

"Okay. I'm still getting used to everything." I settle onto the swaying bench. "I was going to ask…"

I don't want to be too forward, but I need more space. I will never be able to escape my temptation if I remain in the yurt, so close to Sage.

"What is it, Abby?"

"Do you have an extra bedroom in your house?" My cheeks warm as I avoid Susan's questioning gaze. "Could I—?"

She rests her weathered hand on my knee. "I only have the two rooms, my bedroom and Zachary's nursery. You're uncomfortable living in the yurt?"

"The yurt's fine. Nicer than I expected. But…" I build up my courage and finally whisper, "I'm not used to sharing my living space with anyone."

"Oh, you're having a hard time living with Sage."

"I'm sorry. I don't mean to be rude. I—"

"No worries. It's good feedback. Obviously, I need to make the shared accommodations clearer for future volunteers," Susan says. "Has he done anything—"

"No!" I blurt. "He's been friendly and welcoming. This is all about me."

I hope she believes me. I would hate for Susan to think poorly of Sage, when I'm the one who's so messed up. Obviously most volunteers co-reside without difficulty. Why do I have to make *everything* so hard?

"If you ever want to talk…" Susan takes my hand. "Well, I'm always here. One of the benefits of being water-bound."

I'm so ready for this awkward conversation to be done. Maybe if the focus isn't on me, I can slip away soon. "I was wondering about the water transportation. Since this isn't an island, why all the water taxis?"

"It's the cheapest and quickest transportation option." Susan gestures to the thick forest behind the farmland. "The land beyond my property belongs to the national park. It would be a long hike to reach the nearest road."

That gives me an idea. "Do any of the trails reach the farm?"

"My father carved his own trail so we could easily go on bushwalks." Susan quickly explains the directions to the trailhead. "Be careful. You could lose yourself in that wilderness."

Losing myself among the endless acres is exactly what I need.

Two hours later, I'm standing high above the farm. From my vantage point, the green hillside slopes toward the bay. When the land flattens, near the boundaries of Susan's farm, the overgrown wilds turn into the carefully manicured rectangles of the gardens.

From up so high, I can spot the exact point where chaos transforms to neat and tidy order. I relate more to the chaos. Ever since Robbie went away, my life has been nothing but a muddled bundle of disarray.

Susan was wrong. I don't have to worry about losing myself in the wilderness. I'm already lost.

A small part of me yearns for normality, though.

Maybe that's why I'm drawn to Sage.

I hiked so high to escape my attraction and embrace isolation. But on top of this hilltop, I'm still thinking of Sage. The seclusion is no longer comforting, as it had been. Being by myself only highlights my loneliness.

Chapter
5

The breakfast bell's soft chime wakes me. As I rub the sleep from my eyes, I glance over at Sage. He sits propped against the wall, reading a book about meditation. When he notices I'm awake, he quickly closes the book and places it on a small shelf, next to another text on Buddhism.

"Since I'm ready to go, why don't I give you some space to change? Meet you at the tables?"

A loud yawn escapes. "See you in fifteen."

Twenty minutes later, I'm still brushing my hair. When I glance at my watch, I can't believe how much time has passed. Normally, I throw on whatever clothes are the cleanest and most convenient then quickly brush my teeth. I'm lucky if I even take the time to run a brush through my hair.

I wrinkle my nose, throw the brush on the bathroom counter, and muss up my hair a bit. I rush down the trail to the covered breakfast area. Walking so quickly leaves little time to wonder about my radical shift. *Why would I care what Sage thinks of me?*

When I finally reach the tables, Sage reads his book, so engrossed he doesn't even notice me.

"We have oatmeal this morning." Susan points out various bowls that dot the table. "There are fresh peaches and berries, cinnamon sugar, and dried currents and raisins. Fix your bowl however you'd like."

"Wow, this looks incredible." I fill a bowl with oatmeal then add peaches and cinnamon sugar to the top. "I never imagined we'd be getting such delicious meals."

"Cooking's how I get my pleasure." Susan gestures to the empty land around us. "I'm lucky I have the two of you to feed. It would get lonely cooking only for myself."

Zachary peeks his head over Susan's shoulder and shrieks from his backpack.

"Don't worry, no one has forgotten you." Sage leans over just enough to tickle Zachary's toes. "You're just too little to eat much."

Susan turns to two metal carafes. "Sage only drinks green tea, so there's hot water in the first, but I made another carafe of coffee in case you prefer something stronger."

"Thanks." I pour a steaming cup of java. "I'm not fun in the mornings without my caffeine fix."

"Come up to the house if you need anything else." She waves as she heads home.

I settle across from Sage, who continues to read his book. The next few minutes are an exercise in patience. Sage seems to be respecting my need to be alone, but the silence presses on me.

I haven't wanted to talk to anybody in forever. In actuality, it's only been six months. I could even give you the exact last date I initiated a genuine social interaction. That date is emblazoned across my mind. I'll never forget it.

Sage takes a bite, licks his spoon, then turns the page. I watch him for ten agonizingly long minutes before I cannot take another minute of silence.

"That's a different book than you were reading this morning." Cinnamon and peach melt in my mouth as I take my first bite of oatmeal. I cannot believe I'm sitting here, initiating conversations. When I pictured volunteering on a far-away Australian farm, I figured I was signing up for a few months of lovely isolation.

"I usually read a few books at once." He places his book,

something about the Dalai Lama and compassion, cover down.

"Interesting reading choices. Why all the Buddhist stuff?" Guys in my college were too busy going to the next party or hitting on the cutest girl to care about religion. Especially religions from halfway across the world.

Sage reaches for the first carafe, pours steaming water over his tea bag, and studies the clear green liquid. "Australia wasn't my first choice of destinations. If it were up to me, I would have gone to an Asian country. Thailand or Cambodia, maybe."

"What would you have done there?" I take a drink of the rich, pungent coffee.

"They have these Buddhist monasteries that welcome visitors. You can stay for a week or a month and pray and meditate with the monks."

He was different from the guys back home, but I didn't realize *how* different. "You wanted to become a monk?"

He smiles but shakes his head. "Not a monk. I wouldn't have minded studying meditation and yoga techniques with their masters, though."

"What stopped you from going? Was it too expensive?"

Sage takes a long sip of his tea. "My mother's a worrier. She didn't like the idea of my traveling abroad at all, so we comprised. I needed to pick a western, first-world country within a half-hour's reach of a major city."

"Wow, talk about overprotective."

Sage's smile falters. "Yeah, well, she has reasons for worrying so much, so I tried to make her more comfortable with me leaving."

"Ah, such a sweet son." I gaze into his gold-speckled eyes and for a moment cannot look away.

He stares back at me. "I try. Besides, an isolated farm is another great place to practice my meditation. I rarely get interrupted."

Those deep brown eyes are too tempting. I need to focus on why I'm here; losing myself in the hard work of the farm. "So is it digging new garden beds or gathering apples today?"

Sage slides a list in front of me. "Susan leaves a new list every few days. We're free to choose to do the tasks in whatever order we want."

As I finish the last of my oatmeal and coffee, I glance at the short list. Debug tomatoes, add composted manure to the empty beds, harvest melons.

"I'll give you a tip. Whatever we harvest for the day often appears on the menu for the next day."

"Harvesting the melons already seemed like the most appealing choice."

Sage grins. "Glad to hear it. I always end up smelling like crap after working with the compost. It'll be good to save that one for later in the day, after I practice."

"It must be hard to focus on meditation when you smell like the back end of a cow." I can't stop the giggle that escapes.

"Very funny." Sage piles the dishes together then offers me a hand. "Let me show you where the melon beds are."

I hesitate before taking his hand. Rejecting a simple act of kindness would be rude, but I haven't allowed myself to touch anybody in so long. Six months, to be precise.

Sage's warm palm—so different from Robbie's—presses against mine as he helps me up. Sage's fingers bear calluses of hard work, whereas Robbie's fingers were much smoother. Sage's hand radiates warmth to mine, when Robbie's hands were always cold and clammy.

Before I realize it, we're already on the trail to the gardens, and my fingers are still entwined in his. Sage keeps up an easy banter as he walks, and we reach the gardens far too quickly. Or not quickly enough, depending on how you look at it.

Why have I allowed him to hold my hand? The answer comes easily, though. The contact is comforting. If I'm honest, it's *more* than comforting.

I free my hand under the premise of examining the garden beds. Sage gestures to the beds at the far end. Thick, wide-leaved vines grow across the beds and down onto the grass. Each vine lies plump with fruit.

"Watermelons." I run my hands over the large, green-speckled orbs then turn to the next bed, which is filled with rough, brown spheres. "And cantaloupes. How can you tell if they're ripe?"

"They call them 'rock melons' in Australia." Sage squats on

one side. He gently pulls me next to him then holds up one of the fruits, still attached to its vine. "They get a sweet, musky smell when they're ready to be picked."

Sage leans even closer to me, until the melon is the only thing separating our faces. For a moment, I forget to breathe.

"Did you smell it?" he asks.

"Smell what?" I sound dumb, but I'm having so much trouble concentrating on mundane garden tasks with Sage so close. Cantaloupes, or whatever they're called Down Under, are so much less enticing.

His cheeks widen into a smile. Sage's teeth are white, straight, and as perfect as the rest of him. I smile back.

"The rock melon? Could you smell how ripe it was?" He lowers the melon down to the bed.

A bee breaks the spell. It buzzes so close to my face, its downy fuzz brushes against my cheek. I squeal and leap backward.

Sage doesn't even try to hide his laugh. "If you're going to be working out here, you'll have to get used to the pollinators. They're everywhere in the garden, but that's a good thing. Too many places are losing their bee populations."

I wipe at the spot the bee grazed, and my cheeks warm in response. I haven't looked at another guy since meeting Robbie, yet I allow myself to go all speechless and mindless whenever Sage gets close to me.

Maybe that's normal when you're attracted to somebody.

Attracted. The word makes me want to run for my backpack. I yearn for my notebook so I can write my confession. I want to be loyal to Robbie, but I can't even get through a melon-sniffing lesson with Sage.

"I'm going to take care of the tomato plants." Sage hands me two empty baskets. "Fill one with watermelon and the other with the rock melons. I usually leave the full baskets at Susan's kitchen door."

I can't remember how to tell the ripe ones from the not-yet-ready ones. My boy-addled brain has completely failed me. I quickly fill the baskets, choosing random melons from each bed. The one with the prettiest colors, the roundest one, the largest one.

Hopefully, my picking criteria will suffice.

Besides, as soon as I deliver these safely to Susan, I will be free to take a break. I'm in desperate need of my backpack, stationery, and a pen. I have *another* confession to write, after all.

Chapter
6

The next evening, I'm calmer as I hike to dinner. I managed to select solitary tasks all afternoon. Forget hand-over-hand vegetable picking or fruit-sniffing lessons from too-cute boys. I spent the afternoon with an empty garden bed and a shovel.

Sage offered to complete that task, as it was the most physical of the options, but when I noticed the single shovel, I made my choice. Anyone can dig up dirt, after all. With every muscle in my body aching and sore, I could only focus on the job at hand. I abandoned thoughts of Sage, and of Robbie, to the lift, tug, and swing of the shovel.

The moment I set the shovel down, though, they all returned. I ran my hand once over the sweaty mess that used to be my hair and booked it for the shower. I wasn't coming to dinner smelling like the inside of a boys' locker room.

I sit down at the table, across from Sage. His curls are still damp. They frame his face more closely when wet, without their normal lift and bounce. He looks hot both ways. I'm not sure which I prefer.

"I didn't want to come to dinner smelling like a cow's behind."
He grins.

"What's for dinner?" I glance around the still-empty table.

"Susan must be running a few minutes late." No sooner does
Sage finish his sentence than Susan crunches up the trail.

"So sorry I'm behind tonight." Susan sets two covered bowls
on the table. She lifts the cover of the first. "I made a quinoa salad
with fresh, garden veggies."

"My favorite." Sage piles two large scoops on his plate. "Susan,
you are too kind to me."

"I try." She smiles but shakes her head as she uncovers the
second bowl. "I'm sorry about the melon. These melons still
needed a few weeks to ripen. It's fairly bitter, but I couldn't bear to
waste food."

"Bitter?" Sage takes a bite but can't hide his nose wrinkling.

"That bad, huh?" Susan frowns at the cantaloupe. "Sage, could
you give Abby a lesson on how to select ripe melons tomorrow?"

"No problem." He puts down his fork before taking another
bite. "I started the lesson yesterday, but she was a little distracted..."

My cheeks blaze.

"A particularly bothersome bee interrupted us, right, Abby?"
He winks at me.

Sage knows exactly what preoccupied me. I should be
vehemently opposed to any more lessons that involve Sage and
me in close proximity together, but I find myself nodding in
agreement.

"Sorry about the melons," I say. "Sage *was* a great teacher. I just
got a little overwhelmed..."

Sage's grin widens. "Yeah, all those fruits and vegetables can be
mighty overwhelming."

"I better get back to the house." Susan steps back onto the path.
"Zachary will be waking from his nap at any time now. Enjoy your
meal."

As soon as she's out of earshot, Sage places another scoop of
melon on his plate. "After thinking about it, I rather enjoy this
melon."

I need to veer the conversation to something other than my

melon catastrophe. "Tell me about your family." Great. Basic Conversation 101. *How much more pathetic can I get?*

Sage takes pity on me, though. "It's just my mom and me at home."

"No brothers or sisters?"

He looks away for a moment. "Siblings would've been nice, but I'm an only child."

I take a bite of cherry tomato and quinoa. "I feel the opposite. The privacy and solitude of being an only child must be wonderful. I grew up with three brothers, a sister, and not a moment to myself. Even now."

"Even now?" He wrinkles his forehead. "Were you still living with your family before you came to Australia?"

"No, but between the four of them, someone's always calling to check in on me." I glance at my bowl. I'm entering dangerous territory here. "I'm the youngest, so they're all pretty protective."

"Sounds nice. When you're the only one, all the expectations are piled on top of you." He shakes his head. "There's no one else to try if you goof up. It can be suffocating."

"That theory never worked for my parents." I try a bite of the orange melon then pucker up in response. "My siblings all have great careers: My brothers—the professor, the lawyer, and the accountant—and my sister, the doctor. They've left big shoes—really big shoes—to fill."

He glances at my discarded melon. "So am I just a terrible teacher, or is there some other reason you picked unripe melons?"

Is he's flirting with me? In high school, none of the other boys ever flirted, an unspoken, unanimous sign of respect to Robbie. Respect they didn't have for any of the other girls' guys. When I started at Erie U, I shut down any flirting at the first "hello". I couldn't think about flirting back then, with everything I was going through. Everything that Robbie was going through.

I'm left in this awkward place. A part of me—this mystery woman I don't know at all—wants to flirt back, but the loyal, rational side knows I couldn't live with myself if I did.

"Do you want to go on a walk before we head to the yurt?" Sage stacks up the empty dishes into a neat pile. "It's still pretty early."

"That sounds nice," I say, while the rational girl I used to know screams a silent 'No!"

He takes my hand again. I'm so sensitive that his innocent touch sends fireworks shooting up to my elbows.

"Where are we going?" I try to keep my mind focused on the mundane.

He leads me onto a path I haven't explored yet. "Enjoy the mystery. Life is better with surprises."

I can't remember the last time I allowed myself a surprise. For the last few years, I have clung to things I could control and rejected everything else. *But do I have control over anything?*

I couldn't control when Robbie left, after all. I'm failing at controlling my attraction to Sage. I cannot even control the tidal wave of emotions trying to wipe me out. Maybe it would be better to just go along with life and see where it takes me, instead of fighting it every step of the way.

Sage leads me into an open field. The turned soil lies empty, with only the occasional weed growing.

"What grows here?" I ask.

Sage shrugs. "It probably used to be full of some sort of grain, but Susan hasn't planted it for a while."

"I can see why." The field is enormous. It would take a whole crew of farm workers to manage something this size. "So why are we here?"

Sage heads over to a plastic storage bin at the far end of the field. He pulls out a thick, rough blanket, spreads it across the soil, and adds two outdoor cushions. "Star-gazing."

"So this is what you do for fun around here?"

"Look around. What else is there to do?" Sage lies back onto the blanket and stares up at the sky. "Have you looked at the Australian sky before?"

I glance down at the blanket. If only it were three times bigger. When I lie down, I'm going to be *so* close to Sage. But I can't just stand here. Slowly, I lower myself to the blanket.

If I lie on the edge, I have just enough room that my body doesn't touch his. Sage's spicy scent wafts over to me. And I want *more*. I want to press myself so close that his muscular body rests against mine. I want to snuggle up until the only thing I smell is *eau du* Sage. I want to explore his full, pink lips.

My body is betraying me after all this time. I need to stay true—in my heart and mind—to Robbie. I can't do this. It's too much, too close, too soon.

But just as every muscle tenses and I'm ready to flee, Sage takes my hand. With his other hand, he points to the sky. "Look," he whispers.

The tree line ends where the field begins, leaving a wide-open expanse of sky. The night has darkened enough that dozens of stars shine in the sky. Something's different, though, and at first, it's hard to put my finger on what's wrong.

I keep watching. As the night darkens and more stars appear, I finally figure it out. "They're the wrong stars."

"They're the right stars for Australia." He laughs. "But they're different stars than you're used to."

Entirely new constellations twinkle before my eyes. The familiar old stars—the bright North Star, the Big Dipper—are absent. In their place sits a new skyful of stars.

"See those four?" He points to four specific stars that glow more brightly than many of the others. "That constellation's called the Southern Cross."

"I'm surprised you know that." I try to check out the other differences in the sky, but they're hard to pay attention to when Sage rests so close to me. "Most guys your age would be more focused on the latest video game cheats."

"Wasted time," he says. "I'm not going to waste another minute of my life."

His words hit me hard. For the last six months, I've been trying to escape each day through meaningless television shows and novels. Alone and isolated, by choice, I've been on the exact opposite path as Sage. Rather than making the most of each day, I've been trapped in stasis.

A need to rush back to the yurt, to escape from this too-real conversation, floods me. Instead of giving in, though, I fight the urge to self-isolate. The first step is easy; don't get up. Non-action always comes easier than action. The second step will be much harder. Continuing conversation is something with which I am out of practice.

"What do you like about the stars?" I finally ask.

"The backward-ness of the sky reminds me I'm somewhere completely different. It reminds me I'm living life, and when you're living, even something as mundane as looking at the stars becomes novel and intriguing." He squeezes my hand.

Talk about intriguing. I've never met anyone who thinks as deeply as Sage does. In the few conversations we've had, he's challenged me to see the world a whole new way. As much as I want to escape to my safe haven of notebook and purple envelopes, I can't help but think Sage might be right. Maybe I need to start living a little.

I roll toward him. "Thank you."

When he leans in my direction, we're so close, our noses nearly touch. His lips are inches from mine. I can't stop studying them.

"Abby."

I roll completely off the blanket then jump up as I rub soil from my clothing. "It's late. We better get back to the yurt."

He stares quizzically at me for moment then cleans up the blankets and cushions. We hike back to our yurt in complete silence. I can't decide if I am more bothered by my feelings of betrayal or my cowardice about living.

Chapter
7

A week later, I hike down to the isolated boat dock during the grays of dawn. As the sky lightens, the misty outline of buildings appears across the bay. A quick boat ride will bring me back to the small town, and for a moment, I consider escaping.

I can't help but recall Sage's first conversation with me. *What are you running from?*

I had the *most* disturbing dreams last night. I've never been one to remember all my dreams in detail, but this one made an impression on me. It involved Sage. His callused hands, his strong arms, his sun-chapped lips. I had *that* kind of dream.

I couldn't stay in that small round room any longer. Even in his sleep, Sage tempts me. To be honest, I don't fully trust myself around him.

Waiting for the breakfast bell by the water seemed a much safer option. I settle onto the dock as the sunrise paints the water. When the purples and pinks of morning tinge the sky, I cannot delay any longer. I need to write to Robbie.

Thirty minutes later, my notebook sits on my lap, but I've only been able to write two words:

Wander & Roam

Dear Robbie,

I don't even know what else to say. I want to be honest with him. I want to be loyal to him. How can I share my growing attraction to Sage? My heart will *always* belong to Robbie, but after all these months of isolation, my body desires more.

While the farm has more space than I'm used to, I can't escape my strong connection to Sage. I'm drawn to him no matter where I go.

I almost laugh when I think back to how crowded the dorms were. Hundreds of bodies all crammed into one building. Yet I could ignore everyone and focus on my blissful isolation. *How are these acres so confining?*

When the breakfast bell finally sounds, I hurry to the covered eating area. If I'm quick, maybe I can finish my breakfast before Sage even makes his way down here.

"You're up early today." With Zachary on her back, Susan stands at the table, arranging today's choices: yogurt, granola, and bowls of fresh fruits. "I hope you like muesli."

"Muesli?" I had heard the name before but never knew what it was.

"Just a fancy name for fruit and granola over yogurt." Susan fixes herself a bowl, adding three scoops of strawberries to the top. "I've only left the country once. We went on a skiing trip to the Swiss Alps when I was nine. I was too nervous to actually ski, but I've always remembered the delicious breakfasts our hotel served."

"Do you wish you could have traveled more?" After preparing my own bowl, I try a bite. The sweet berries contrast with the granola's crunch and the yogurt's tart bite.

"I'm satisfied with the life I've created here. I've always been a bit of a homebody, so staying on the farm and taking care of Zachary satisfies me." She smiles as she rubs his little foot, the only part of him she can reach. "Besides, I get to listen to stories from all the travelers that spend a few weeks on my farm. Since I've signed up to be a WWOOFing host, I get to experience exotic places by proxy."

While Susan appears satisfied with listening to the tales of her volunteers, others' stories must be a sad substitute for actually being able to travel. To immerse oneself in the smells, tastes, sounds, and experiences of a new culture. I've been living life in a similar way, though. Hiding away in my own secluded corner of the world—my old dorm—without joining in the activities all around me.

For a long time, I thought I was protecting myself. Perhaps I was merely extending my pain. Sage's words from last night have echoed on my brain: *I'm not going to waste another minute of my life.*

Maybe I'm done wasting minutes. Maybe I'm ready to start living. It's so tempting, but the thought of Robbie makes me question everything again and again.

"Good morning, Sunshine." Sage walks to the table. He must have just left the shower. A towel's draped around his neck, and he carries his shirt. That's right, he's wearing absolutely no shirt at all. I stare at him for a moment, unable to take my eyes off the water droplets falling from his wet curls onto his bronze-hued shoulders. The droplets weave their way down his body, some winding around his muscular arms and others tracing a path on his smooth, golden chest.

"Where'd you disappear to this morning?" He fills his bowl completely to the top with all the fixings. "I heard you tossing and turning, then you were just gone."

He heard me last night? I become engrossed in scraping my bowl into the compost bucket. I hope I didn't verbalize any part of my dream. I can't even imagine how awkward that would be.

"I was in the mood for a walk." No need to tell him where I was walking. Best leave *that* information to myself, in case I need to hide another morning.

"Morning, Sage." Susan collects all the breakfast materials onto a tray after ensuring we've had all we want. "Unfortunately, I need you to rototill the left side of the field today. I want to try my luck at growing a new grain next year."

"No problem. I've seen the machine in the shed." He grins. "I'll be finished by lunchtime."

"You're *such* a help." Susan mouths her thanks again to Sage.

"Abby, could you fill two baskets with cucumbers? I'm ready to start pickling today."

"No problem." I help her gather the last of the breakfast dishes. "I'll have those to you by lunch."

Susan leaves, and Sage and I sit across the table from one another. Since the dishes are all gone, I can't even ignore him under the pretense of eating and drinking.

"Disappointing how we're going to work alone today," he says. "I've grown used to having you by my side this week."

"Having some space can be nice, too." But I'm just as sad. I thought I'd look forward to long, solitary hours in the garden, but I've grown to love his playful bantering. Sage can make even the most tedious gardening tasks entertaining.

"I have an idea." Sage beams at me. "Why don't you join me after lunch?"

Every day after lunch, Sage disappears from the gardens. I assume this is when he's doing his "practice", as he calls it. He has guarded his privacy fiercely, never allowing anyone to come along or interrupt him.

Why invite me to join him now?

I'm so nervous, I immediately want to decline his offer. But when I open my mouth, the only word that comes out is, "Yes."

"Perfect. Let's meet here for lunch and then you can hike with me." Sage gives a friendly wave, finally pulls on his shirt, and sets off toward Susan's tool shed.

I'm left alone at the table with my ever-building guilt. It would have been so much safer to keep our distance for the entire day. I could blame my rash words on a whole bunch of factors, but it comes down to a single reason.

I want to spend more time with him. Something about Sage calls to me. I have a feeling I'm going to be in trouble after lunch. But I'm far too excited about my Sage-time rendezvous to consider the consequences.

Chapter
8

Sage meets me for lunch. He unpacks our sandwiches, turkey for me and vegetarian for him, along with small bags of fresh fruits and veggies. "I can't believe you actually said yes." Sage grins at me before taking a bite of his sandwich.

"Why is that surprising?" I can't meet his eyes. "Do I seem that unfriendly?"

"Not unfriendly. More like… cautious." Sage studies me while I meticulously examine my sandwich. "Like somebody's hurt you before."

Just like that, he cuts to the crux of the matter. I *am* cautious. I *have* been hurt before. *How can he read me so well?*

"H-have you ever been hurt?" I finally ask. Anything to get his attention off me.

"Do you mean, hurt by a girl?" The corners of his mouth rise up.

I force myself to ask him the question that's been on my mind all day. "Do you have a girlfriend?"

"Do you have a boyfriend?"

He had to ask the question I've been dreading. I've practiced my answer, and I only hope the multiple times I recited it to myself help make my answer sound real. "I... I used to."

"So we're both free—" My expression must have been pretty interesting to stop him mid-sentence. "Free to hike now. Are you ready?"

I try to decide between escaping to the isolation of our yurt and accompanying Sage. Going to the yurt would be the safest choice, but Sage tempts me with his eager smile.

"I've been thinking about this all day," he whispers as we hike. So have I, which is exactly why I'm in trouble.

Sage leads me higher and higher up a rocky trail, until white sailboats dotting the far-away bay appear. He stops next to a large, flat rock overlooking the water and climbs on top of it. After settling in a cross-legged position, he gestures for me to sit across from him.

"Best view within walking distance of the farm." He waits for my reaction.

"Do you come here often?" I'm curious about where he always disappears.

"Every day. This is my favorite place to meditate."

I can see why. The tree cover breaks just enough to allow rays of sun to stream down on the rock. The water sparkles. This could be the most peaceful spot on the farm.

"So, what do you think?" he asks.

"Flat rock is a pretty amazing place."

"Flat rock? That does not capture the specialness." He shakes his head, over-exaggerating his disappointment. "We definitely need to come up with a better name."

"Seeing as how I don't even know how to meditate..."

Sage claps his hands together. "That's it! You need a lesson in the 'now.'"

I can't hold in my sigh. "I don't even believe in that 'now' stuff."

"There's nothing to believe in. It's just something you need to experience." A grin spreads across his face. "Please? Try it once?"

I wonder what the harm would be. Meditating can't hurt. It could even help. "Okay."

"Okay? As in yes?" He leans closer.

"Yes, I'll try your 'now' stuff." I hurry to set up rules and boundaries for our experiment. "I'll try it *once*. Don't think I'm going to start eating that vegan junk or praying to the Buddha."

Sage laughs. "You don't pray to Buddha. It's more—"

If he starts talking philosophy, it will be dark before we hike down the butte. "I just need the rules for how to be present."

"Rule Number One: let your body experience what's happening in the moment, and *embrace* those feelings. It won't work if you're thinking about the future or the past. You *have* to remain in the moment." His face grows more serious. "Rule Number Two: radical honesty."

"Radical honesty?" The phrase scares me before I even know what it means.

"Full and total honesty." He watches me, as if he suspects this might be the hardest part of our experiment.

I make a face. "I'm not sure I can be fully honest." Even talking about radical honesty makes my heart race. I'm not ready to share all of my secrets.

"What if you only had to be honest with yourself?"

Relief flows through me. "I think I can manage that." As long as I don't have to share anything about Robbie, or how I came to this Australian farm, I can manage. I should be able to be open with myself. It can't be that hard.

Sage scoots closer until we sit knee to knee. He reaches for my hand. "Like this." As he places it palm-up against my knee, he brushes his thumb gently along my palm. I quickly flip the other hand over, eager to avoid his soft touch. He rests his hands on his knees then whispers, "Just be."

I sit and wait. Unsure of what is supposed to happen, I focus on my body. The sun shines down on my face and the back of my arms, creating pleasant warmth. A gentle breeze blows strands of hair across my forehead. My fingertips graze against Sage's, creating fiery tingles.

While I look everywhere but up, Sage watches me the entire

time. I slowly meet his gaze. The corners of his mouth turn up slightly. His eyes crinkle, and a full smile emerges. He could be playing connect-the-dots with the freckles on my nose and cheeks. I squirm just the tiniest bit.

"What are you feeling?" he asks.

What an unusual question. Most people ask *how* others are feeling, seeking definitive answers. Sage has posed a more open-ended question, though. "The sun feels amazing."

"Your freckles are cute. I like all thirty-seven of them."

I gasp. He *was* counting! "I could look at the boats for hours. It's so peaceful watching them sail."

"I love the breeze. I especially love the way the wind is blowing your hair around," he whispers.

This radical honesty is way more personal than I was expecting. I pause, thinking how to respond.

Sage shakes his head, his wild locks bouncing with his movement. "Don't think. Just be."

"I like the way our fingers feel together. I don't want to separate them."

Before I can even wonder how *that* escaped my mouth, Sage moves his hands closer, interlocking our fingers. "I don't want you to move them, either."

I cannot stop staring into Sage's chestnut-hued eyes. I'm not going to share *that* thought, though. Not trusting myself, I remain silent.

He leans close. "I want to kiss you."

"I want to kiss you, too," I whisper before clenching my lips together.

Sage brushes his lips against mine. His sun-scorched roughness caresses my lip-glossed softness. After one light kiss, he eases back.

"More," I whisper. This time, my lips are the ones to seek his.

Beneath the warmth of the sun, alongside the gentle breeze and overlooking the scenic bay, our mouths meet. He tastes of mint-tinged sweetness. His tongue dances with mine, and our lips crush together. All the while, my fingers tingle as they remain interlocked with his upon our knees.

With a small groan, Sage breaks away. "Welcome to the 'now', Abby."

I've never kissed anyone other than Robbie. All this time, I've stayed loyal to him, no matter how big our troubles became. My throat tightens, and my eyes well. *Forgive me, Robbie.*

"Abby?" Sage strokes my cheek.

The spell is broken. I jump up then hurry back to the path.

"Wait for me. What did you think?" Sage gathers his backpack and catches up to me.

I liked it, and that's the worst part of this mess. I liked kissing Sage. I swallow and blink my eyes to keep the tears from falling.

He touches my shoulder. "What's wrong? Talk to me."

Determined not to cry, I move a little faster down the trail. "Was that one of your moves? I have to admit, that was pretty slick."

"You think I have moves?" Sage grins. "No, that was fully experiencing life in the present."

I should have never agreed to try one of Sage's silly meditations. My body was obviously confused after being alone for so long.

Sage hums as he hikes. The happy tune wears at the last of my patience until I grab a small pebble and flick it at him.

"Ouch! Are you actually mad at me?"

He knows I've been hurt. He mentioned it at lunch. With each step down the hill, my body grows tenser.

When I don't respond, he adds, "You wanted to kiss me just as much as I wanted to kiss you. Remember, I'm the one who stopped the smooching."

I glare back at him.

"And FYI... you are the *only* one I have meditated with."

I toss another pebble.

"Radical honesty," he calls before ducking once more.

Chapter
9

I barely make it through the next morning's chores before the need to write another letter overwhelms me. I try to focus on today's final tasks to escape the rush of feelings that threaten to break loose. As soon as I harvest the last of the zucchini, I grab my notebook and favorite pen.

> *I have a confession to make. I kissed Sage yesterday. Even worse, I liked kissing him. It wasn't planned. If he or I had tried to plan it, the kiss would have never happened. I would have kept control.*
>
> *Robbie, it's just not fair that we can't be together. If you were here, I would have never been tempted to kiss another boy. You and me. It was always you and me. If the world were fair, we would have been the ones kissing yesterday.*
>
> *I can hear your voice telling me to be happy. You aren't mad at all about the stolen kiss, are you? Well, I am angry with myself. I wanted so badly to stay loyal to you.*
>
> *But I'm failing.*

Extra XXXXXOOOOOO
Abby

"You liked kissing me? I *knew* it!" Sage snatches the letter from me.

Before I can spin around, he dashes away, still holding my precious letter. "Sage, give me back my letter."

"Catch me first," he calls from one of the trails.

"I am *not* playing tag!" I scream into the wind. Hot tears escape, but they do nothing to cool my blazing cheeks. I sink to the grass, cover my face, and focus on breathing.

Moments later, crisp paper rubs against my hands. Sage crouches in front of me, holding my letter out. For once, he isn't smiling. "Listen, I really messed up." He runs his hand through his hair and looks away. "I was just trying to goof around. I didn't mean to upset you."

"Or completely invade my privacy?"

"That too. I peeked at your 'I liked kissing Sage' line and your radical honesty overwhelmed me."

I pick up the closest thing I can find—my backpack—and whack him with it.

"Abby, I really am sorry." He sounds so sincere that I believe him.

I wipe away the last of my tears. Typically, I'm able to hold in my emotions. The last time I *really* cried was the last night I spent with Robbie. Not a tear has fallen since that day. Until now.

"Who's Robbie?"

Of all the questions, this is the hardest one for me to answer. I don't talk about Robbie. It just hurts too much. "Why won't you talk about the future?" I snap. Two can play this game.

Sage turns away but not quickly enough to hide the shudder that passes through his body. "Touché."

"We promised. I won't ask about the future, and you won't bring up the past." We face away from one another; I watch the gardens while he stares into the forest.

"Just the 'now'?" he asks.

I nod as calm washes over me.

Sage heads off for his daily disappearing spell. "What if the 'now' isn't enough?" he whispers.

"It has to be." But no one is left to hear my quiet words.

Yesterday was mind-blowingly wonderful. The meditation, the words we shared, our kiss, filled a hole that has been empty for so long. I wasn't angry with Sage. No, I was furious with myself. I committed the ultimate betrayal. For the entire time we were in the present, I didn't think once of Robbie.

Chapter
10

I arrive at the dock as the sun begins to rise. I have my new schedule down. Wake early and walk down to the docks, complete my volunteer hours after breakfast, then explore the park's hiking trails until dinner. I usually bring along a paperback and search for a cozy reading spot along the trail.

I came here to volunteer after all, not to flirt with good-looking boys.

Luckily, Susan's plan to prepare the field has worked in my favor. Sage underestimated how long it would take him to till the hard, rocky soil. During the last few days, he worked in the field while I cared for the vegetables.

I've finished five entire novels and hiked an impossible-to-calculate number of miles. The rugged trails aren't marked with mile markers. Plus, that tricky kilometer to mile conversion makes it even more difficult to figure out distances.

I'm tiring of my self-imposed isolation though.

I still haven't mastered vegetable gardening, and I hate to bother Susan with my endless questions. She's already so busy with caring for Zachary, cooking meals for us, and preserving the harvest. The last thing she needs is my twenty questions about every task.

If I'm honest, I don't just miss Sage's patience in answering my gardening questions. I miss his silly jokes and his philosophical discussions. I think of his kind smile and over-the-top optimism way more than I should.

This scares me. I used to think that I was only physically attracted to him, but my feelings are bigger than that. It was easy to dismiss physical attraction. It's much harder to ignore the budding friendship we were developing.

Footsteps crunch down the leafy path, sounding louder and louder. When they still, I turn away from the bay. Sage waits where the wooden planks meet the soil.

Speak of the devil. If devils could be that cute and kind.

"I finally found your hiding spot." He walks across the short dock. "Can I join you?"

I nod and turn back to the water. "I wasn't hiding—"

"Hiding, running, avoiding." He pulls off his shoes then sits next to me, placing his feet in the water. "Call it whatever you want."

I can't keep denying his words. He's right, after all. How does he know me so well?

For the next few minutes, the only sound is of Sage's splashing feet. I try to think of something to say, but I can't find the words. I'm not even sure how to respond. *Do I apologize for over-reacting to the kiss?* I can't stop replaying that moment in my mind. I certainly don't want to talk about it.

I could just explain why growing close to someone is so hard. But that would mean talking about Robbie. I'm not ready. I can't say his name or tell our story without drudging up a torrent of feelings.

Silence is certainly the easiest response. Maybe he'll give up and go away. Leave me to my misery.

Sage sighs. "I'm sorry, Abby."

An apology? That certainly wasn't what I was expecting. "Why? What do you have to be sorry for?"

"I didn't mean to push you," he says. "You've been through a lot."

"How do you *know* that?" I turn so I'm facing him.

"It's kind of obvious." He pulls his feet from the water and faces me.

His words sting. Do I really look that broken? I study my lap, unable to look at him.

"Sorry, I wasn't trying to be rude." He places one finger under my chin and raises my head until our eyes meet. "If you ever want to talk about what happened, I'm here. I've been told I'm a pretty good listener."

"Thanks, but I'm not…"

"Not ready. I get it, but can we go back to being friends?" He pauses. "I miss you."

I miss him too. Even during this awkward conversation, I'm just glad he's *here*.

"I'd like that." Feeling brave, I add, "A lot."

Sage grins. As always, his smile lights up his face. "Should we get breakfast? I finished the field so we actually get to work together today."

As we hike back to the picnic tables, I can't help smiling. I've spent too much of this past year alone. I'm ready for friendship. Maybe with time, I'll even be ready for more.

Chapter
11

Over breakfast, Susan does not give us her daily list of chores. "The raspberries are ripe, and the lorikeets have been flocking, waiting to snatch whatever berries they can. We're going to spend the day canning."

"Canning?" The term conjures up memories of the Amish farms back in Ohio. "We're going to make jam?"

Sage groans and rubs his stomach. "I'm picturing tomorrow's breakfast already."

"I have to warn you. Canning is a tedious chore that's going to take the entire day," Susan says.

The nice thing about being on the farm, away from the rush of school and friends, is that I have nothing better to do. "What do you need us to do first?"

Susan grabs eight white buckets off the highest shelf and hands them to us. "Fill these with the ripe berries then meet me back in the kitchen."

ANNA KYSS

The sweet-tart smell of raspberries fills the air as we pick. The sun's warmth and the breeze waft the berry fragrance around even more. At the university, I once wondered why anyone would settle for manual labor, but now I understand the rewards. The slight ache in my muscles satisfies me, as one by one each bucket brims with berries. While picking, I have been able to shut off my thinking and focus solely on the task at hand.

"You're taking this job way too seriously," Sage calls, popping a handful of berries into his mouth. "I haven't seen you sample one single berry."

"We aren't getting paid to eat all of Susan's berries," I call back.

"We aren't getting paid at all." Sage munches on more berries. His words are only somewhat true. When WWOOFing, you aren't paid in money but in free accommodations and meals.

"Maybe Susan will let us take home some of the jam. It would make great presents for next Christmas."

Sage squeezes his eyes shut, and his smile disappears.

I can't imagine what I said that would be that distressing. "Are you upset about missing this Christmas with your family?"

He blinks away whatever is wrong and crosses over to my row. "I'm pained that you're missing the true delight of berry picking—eating a sun-ripened berry right off the bush." Sage plucks a berry and holds it to my mouth between fuchsia-stained fingers. "One of life's true pleasures."

I hesitate, staring at the puckered berry to avoid his gaze.

"When will you have another chance to eat an Australian raspberry just after it's been picked? Seize the moment, Abby."

Slowly, I take the berry into my mouth. My lips brush gently across his fingertip. As I close my eyes, warmth and sweetness explode in my mouth. Sage was right. This is hands-down the best raspberry I have ever eaten.

"So? What do you think?" He watches me carefully.

"Yum!" I carefully control my reaction.

"That's it? 'Yum'? Clearly, you need to try one more." He offers another berry to me.

The next few hours pass quickly, between berry-tasting, laughter, and some actual work. We manage to fill up every white bucket, and by lunchtime, we haul the last two buckets to the kitchen.

He sets down his bucket then grabs for mine. His fingers move softly down the back of my hands until they reach the handle. Sage has been openly flirting with me since I tasted that first berry. I'm not sure whether it's due to the sugar or the sunshine, but I don't mind. Our fingers crisscross over the handle, and our eyes meet.

"Oh good, you're back." Susan sets two plates on her kitchen table. "Why don't you snack on some sandwiches while I start jamming?"

By the time we finish eating, the berries bubble in three enormous pots. Susan measures sugar with one hand while she stirs with the other. "Good timing. I'm glad you came back before Zachary wakes from his nap. It's so hard to get anything accomplished when he's awake."

The sounds of a baby wailing punctuate her words.

"You jinxed yourself," Sage teases.

"You're right. Never mention a sleeping baby." Susan pulls off her berry-splattered apron. "I need to nurse him. Can you stir these pots until I return? They need constant mixing so the jam doesn't burn."

"Don't worry. We'll watch over it," I say.

She rinses her hands. "If the sauce starts to gel together, turn down the heat."

"Go feed your baby," Sage calls as Susan heads upstairs. He looks at the two clean aprons then ties on the strawberry-dotted one.

"Pink is a good look on you." I put on the remaining apron—a black-and-yellow checkerboard with tiny bumblebees flying along the border.

Sage mixes the jam then dips one of the tasting spoons into the bubbling mixture. He lets the reddish-pink sauce drip back into the pan. After blowing on the spoon, he holds the warm metal to my nose, dotting it with a sticky pink circle. "Pink is a good look on you, too."

Sage grasps both my upper arms when I grab the spoon. "No double-dipping," he whispers before lowering his mouth. My lips wait—eagerly—for the kiss that has been building up all day. I close my eyes, and he licks my nose. "Tasty," he says between laughs.

"We should test it again," I whisper back.

"Wouldn't want the jam to burn." Sage hands me a clean spoon.

I stir, test, blow, then hold the still-warm spoon above Sage's nose. He lifts his face as I lower the spoon, and I accidentally paint his lips with the raspberry-scented mixture.

"Wow, I'm kind of disappointed that cooking isn't one of our duties. I like how feisty you get with your apron on," he says, his mouth sticky. "When I got you messy, I helped you clean up."

"But you moved!" Placing my hands on his shoulders, I raise myself up.

Sage remains completely still. "So? Susan will be back any minute. Do you really want to leave all this evidence?" His lips glisten with pink jam. He smells like sun-kissed raspberries. I can't help but lean closer.

Zachary's baby talk loudens. Shoot, Susan really is on her way back to the kitchen. I swipe the back of my hand over his lips, wiping away every trace of jam.

He turns back toward the pots, dutifully stirring. "I feel cheated," he whispers.

"How's the jam coming?" Susan places Zachary in his highchair with a handful of Cheerios to snack on.

While she's distracted, I subtly try to clean my hand on the bottom of my apron. My efforts leave a telltale pink smear. It barely matters. I probably wear my guilt on my face, anyway. I came *way* too close to kissing Sage. If we were alone for another few minutes, I probably would have given in to the temptation. Again.

When we maintain our distance, I'm rational and in control. But every time I get close to Sage, my brain shuts off and my body goes on autopilot. I don't like the course it's taking, though. Or maybe, I like it too much.

"I think it's done. You should come check it." Sage stirs continuously as if nothing happened.

That familiar pressure to write—no, confess—returns, but I don't have time to focus on it. Sterilized jars wait to be filled, lidded, and steamed until they seal. We wipe clean jar after jar until dozens of glistening jams line Susan's table and counters.

"Thank you for putting in so many extra hours." Susan hands us a bag stuffed with dinner foods. "Why don't you take this weekend off in appreciation?"

The exhaustion of today's work makes a weekend to myself tempting.

"We could go to the city. Have you seen Sydney yet?" Sage asks.

"No, I came straight from the airport." This wasn't a tourist trip, after all.

"We have one of the most beautiful cities in the world," Susan says. "It would be a tragedy if you didn't see some of the sights during your stay."

"So it's decided. We'll spend tomorrow in Sydney," Sage says.

It's decided? Did I miss the part where I agreed? While a part of me wants to argue the decision, another part is completely tempted by an entire day to spend together. I've spent as much time feeling confused this month as I have harvesting vegetables.

Sage hands me the dinner bag. "I'll be up in a few minutes. I just need to talk with Susan for a moment."

I silently approve the plan when I accept the food bag without complaint. The entire hike up to our yurt is spent contemplating what my decision means. Tomorrow, I'll spend the day with Sage. The *entire* day. We won't be picking vegetables, shoveling mulch, or doing any other distracting farm chores.

We'll spend the day riding the ferries, seeing the sights, and enjoying one another. Almost like a date. That one thought sours everything. Tonight, I will write away my guilt and tuck it inside one of the remaining purple envelopes.

Chapter 12

When I wake up Saturday, Sage is nowhere to be seen. Odd. I fill my backpack with the essentials then head to the dining area. Susan waits with a small paper bag.

She tucks the bag into my backpack then pulls the zipper securely. "You'll find raspberry scones for breakfast. You can nibble on them while on the ferry."

"Where is Sage? Have you seen him?"

"Oh, he took the first boat over as soon as the sun rose. He said to meet him at Cuppa's." Zachary leans to the side of his wrap. His smiling face peeks from behind Susan's back. "It's just a block from the ferry docks."

"Why—?"

"You'd have to ask Sage. I don't want to spoil all his surprises," Susan says. "You might want to pack a change of clothes in your backpack."

"Why? I'll be back tonight." I had *better* return this evening. I spent the entire night preparing myself to spend the day with Sage. I could make it twelve hours, but my willpower's never going to last all night long.

"Better safe than sorry." She shoos me onto the trail. "You never know when the ferry schedule's going to run wonky."

When I get back to the yurt, I throw some extra clothes in my backpack then hurry to the bathroom to grab my toiletries. The water taxi must be waiting for me by now.

As I hike down to the water's edge, I can't help but wonder about Sage's absence. *Since we were both visiting Sydney, why not catch a ride together?*

An hour later, I pull open the door to Cuppa's. The aromatic smell of roasted coffee beans fills the air. As soon as I place my latte order, I spot Sage at a corner table.

"Why did you ditch me?" I settle across from him in the cozy booth.

"Ditch you? I left at the crack of dawn to get everything ready." He sips his steaming drink.

What kind of things need to be prepared for a day trip into the city? While part of me wants to question him more, the other part just wants to enjoy the day. If Sage needs to take charge, that's fine. I don't even know what Sydney has to offer.

"No wonder you wanted to meet at a coffee house..." I pause when the barista brings me my latte. "You must need a four-shot java boost if you woke that early."

"I don't touch that crap... anymore." Sage pushes his cup toward me. It's full of pale green liquid. "I only drink green tea."

I've wondered about it each morning, but I haven't found a polite way to ask. I guess I'll just be blunt. "Why tea?"

He doesn't seem offended by my probing questions. "It's filled with antioxidants and loads of other good stuff."

"Oh, so this is more of your health nut thing." I take a long gulp of coffee. I'll take loads of caffeine and sugar any day.

Sage flinches. "Hey, we need to catch our ferry in fifteen minutes. We'd better head to the docks."

We finish our drinks, pull on our backpacks, and head out the door. We reach the docks in less than five minutes. Only a few storefronts dot the tiny town, and the streets are nearly empty.

The ferry's bell tolls as soon as we sit on a nearby bench. Within minutes, the boat docks and a line of passengers slowly steps aboard. After we show our weekend passes, Sage leads me up the ramp and to the side of the boat. I glance at the windows behind me. Most of the ferry-goers have gathered inside.

"Trust me, you'll love the view when we approach Sydney." He sits down first and pats the bench next to him.

I place my backpack between my feet and settle next to Sage as the ferry takes off. The sun already blazes in the sky, but the breeze takes the heat's edge away. After pulling a bottle of sunscreen from my bag, I rub it into my arms, legs, and face. Sage ignores the passing scenery and focuses his attention entirely on me.

"What? I left Susan's too early to finish my morning routine." A white sunscreen glob slowly slides down my back, but no matter which way I stretch, I cannot reach it.

"Let me." Sage turns me until I'm half-sitting on the narrow bench and half-supporting myself with my right foot. His warm hands press against my back, above my sundress. They stretch and pull my skin, rubbing until the sunscreen is completely absorbed. Yet he doesn't stop. His thumbs rub my taut upper back muscles while his fingers stroke from my neck to my shoulders. I can't remember the last time someone focused entirely on my comfort. Maybe never.

I'm not saying Robbie wasn't kind and thoughtful, but he had too much of his own stuff going on. I close my eyes and relax into Sage's touch.

"Look at the view," he whispers into my ear. I open my eyes to spot the ferry gliding past the Sydney skyline.

I stand alongside the boat's railing, away from Sage's magic hands, and point to the iconic white building featured on nearly every picture of Sydney. "That's the Opera House, right?"

"You guessed it—Sydney's famous Opera House. Check this out…" Sage digs through his backpack until he finds a postcard and holds it up. The Opera House, the bridge, the boats, all match up perfectly.

The ferry's speaker crackles. "Next stop, Circular Quay. Everyone must depart."

We let the hurried passengers disembark before we approach the ramp. After all, we have the entire day in the city with absolutely nothing planned. After following the last stragglers off the boat, Sage and I walk around the busy waterfront. A street performer rolls a glass orb up and down his body. He rolls the clear ball in impossible directions and appears to levitate it at times.

"So, what do you want to do?" Sage guides me away from the performer.

I shrug. "I have no idea. I don't know anything about Sydney."

"You really flew all the way Down Under without even reading about it?"

"Silly, huh?"

Sage pulls a guidebook from his backpack. "I have a few things I want to do in the evening. Why don't you pick how we'll spend our day?"

The guidebook has to be at least a thousand pages long. I don't want to waste our time reading the entire thing. To be honest, I'm overwhelmed just looking at it. WWOOFing seemed like the perfect choice because I didn't need to make many decisions. I just show up at the farm and follow orders.

I flip open the book, which focuses on Sydney. The page reads, "Darling Harbour: Sydney's primo destination for leisure and entertainment". The guidebook goes on to detail the fancy shops, fine dining, and array of tourist activities the harbor has to offer. We can spend the day shopping, eating, and doing the tourist thing.

One time, Robbie joined us on our family vacation. After two months of relentless asking, my parents caved. Robbie could come, with the stipulation he slept in a different room, with my brothers, and I could vacation plan my heart out. Robbie loved country music, so I chose Nashville. I found an enormous hotel near the Grand Ole Opry, with dozens of restaurants, even more stores, and acres of inside gardens. Everything worked out perfectly. We went to a different restaurant each night, listened to loads of music, and didn't have to walk much, which helped Robbie.

"I can't wait to see what you choose," Sage says softly. "A person's vacation choices tell a lot about them."

ANNA KYSS

His voice snaps me back to my surroundings. *What am I
thinking, planning the same exact activities as my last trip—my only
trip—with Robbie?* No, I need to think of something completely
different, something with no reminders or memories. Something I
could never do with Robbie.

I close the book and look around. A massive bridge rises above
the other buildings in the distance. Tiny objects appear to move
up the bridge's pylons. When I squint, the objects transform into
people. *People.* People climb that enormous bridge.

The metal bridge spans the entire harbor. Climbing the
monster must involve a whole bunch of daring and athleticism. I
would never be able to climb like that with Robbie.

Perfect.

"Well?" Sage paces restlessly. "Are you ready to surprise me?"

"That." I point to the bridge. "I want to do that."

"Walk across the bridge?" Sage glances at his map then leads
me toward the bridge. "There's a walkway right along the road. We
should get some great pictures from the bridge."

The corners of my mouth turn up. "Um, walking sounds a
little boring. Wouldn't the photos be even better from higher up?"

The look on his face is priceless. I wish I had a camera to
capture how his jaw drops and his eyes widen. "You want to do the
climb?" he asks incredulously.

"That's what I was hoping—"

"I never pegged you for an adventure sports kind of girl." Sage
increases the pace. "Climbing the bridge was one of my top three
picks for Sydney, but I figured I'd stop back on my own to complete
it."

My radical deviation from normal vacation activities is paying
off. Sage is happy, and I'm going to be too scared and distracted
even to think about someone else. "What were your other top
picks?"

"You'll find out this evening. We're doing both of them." Sage
turns to me, places his hands around my waist, and spins me.
"We're going to climb the Harbour Bridge!"

We race hand-in-hand to the bridge's climbing office. I barely
notice the renovated stores and hotels that surround the enormous

bridge. It's really, *really* tall. And Sage was wrong. I'm not an adventure-sport type girl. The looming bridge terrifies me.

But it'll help me forget. It isn't too much to ask for one day of peace. For the guilt and the memories and the weight to be lifted for twenty-hour hours. Please, let me enjoy Sydney.

Chapter
13

An hour later, I'm squeezing the skinny rails of a frail-looking catwalk. One step at a time. That's what I've been telling myself for the last thirty minutes as we moved up, up, up. Though we're nearing the apex of the bridge, we still haven't reached it.

Sage walks in front of me. I insisted, so he wouldn't see my hesitation at each new step and my death grip on the railings. Every few minutes, he turns around to smile, point out something far below, or wave. Thinking about how ridiculous we look in our matching full-body, gray-and-blue regulation jumpsuits helps keep a grin on my face. I don't want Sage to waste his climb worrying about me. Besides, I sort of enjoy the new adventurous persona. Maybe I'll even grow into it.

We're nearing another set of stairs. While my logical brain knows they would never send hundreds of tourists a day onto a rickety, faulty structure, my anxiety-fueled thoughts cannot wrap around how the see-through mesh steps can actually be sturdy. I glimpse down at the waves kicked up by a boat's wake and press my lips together.

The upward progression stops, and group members pause for photos as they reach the apex one by one. This leaves me stuck on the stairs. I glance at my tether, locked into a steel cable that runs alongside the catwalks and stairs. Supposedly, the tethers should keep us safe, but I struggle with how this skinnier-than-my-finger rope is supposed to fight the powerful force of gravity.

"Coming?" Sage holds out his hand. He's next in line to step onto the highest catwalk.

My white knuckles firmly grasp the side. The warm metal provides mild reassurance. As long as I don't let go, I shouldn't fall. I'm unsure if a person can ever provide the same promise of safety. Maybe that's my problem. *If I refuse to trust anyone again, how will I ever move on?* Slowly, I release the rail then reach for the security of his fingers. Hand-in-hand, we take the final steps to the top.

Our group walks down the long catwalk, posing for perfect photos in front of the Opera House. The guide moves from family to couple to solo traveler, snapping memories of their bravery. A wind gust catches me off guard, and I grip even tighter.

"Ouch!" Sage says, but he smiles at me. When I try to release his hand, he pulls me to him and holds me securely.

When he wraps his arms around me, my hesitation and fear fade away. Up here, it's Sage and I and our sky-high adrenaline. My ground-level worries don't even register. Sage's embrace is so comforting, all I can think about it how I want *more*.

"Adventurous must be the new sexy," he says as his lips caress mine.

"Don't stop," I plead.

We kiss—frantically at first, then slowly and sweetly. I barely notice the three wire cords digging into my back, the people around us, or the growing breeze. My attention's entirely on Sage's muscular arm, so firm beneath my hand, his warm body so snug against mine. His distracting lips, which haven't stopped moving.

A bright flash of light interrupts our moment. "That will be a great photo. They'll be available for purchase at the base for only $19.99."

I open my eyes to find myself pressed against the side of the catwalk, between thin cords and Sage's strong body.

"You can't get more 'now' than that," Sage whispers in my ear. "Abandoning your fears to the pleasures of the moment? Wicked hot."

I carefully step to the middle of the catwalk, about a half-inch of movement. "So you weren't afraid at all?"

"I had to learn to manage my fear a while ago." Sage's smile fades, and his entire face darkens. "Imagined fears are nothing compared to that."

Before I can ask him what he means, Sage gestures to the departing group and hurries after them. I begin my slow, careful descent from the bridge. *Imagined fears.* Thinking about it that way, the journey down isn't nearly so hard.

When we reach the bottom of the bridge, I spot a restroom and sigh with relief. "Bathroom break?"

Sage nods. "I need to do something. Can you wait for me right here?"

After using the bathroom, I take an extra minute to peek in the mirror, run a brush through my windswept hair, and reapply lip gloss. I've probably looked in a mirror twice as often these last few weeks. Before I can agonize over whether it's a good thing or a bad thing, I head out to find Sage.

He still isn't back. After settling on a nearby bench, I pull the guidebook out of my backpack. Flipping through the pages, I scan activity after activity.

"My turn." Sage closes the book and tucks it away. "I know exactly what we're doing next. Are you ready?"

I follow him along the waterfront. "Do I get a hint?"

"Nope." He grins. "Thinking about what's to come takes you out of the moment."

We're approaching the Opera House again, and its white sail-like roof mimics the boats that soar by in the water. What a beautiful city. Sydney is vibrant, alive, and so different from the Midwest's dying cities. The sun beats down from the bluest of skies, warming everything around me. Between Sage's intense stare and his sexy smile, my inside temperature soon matches the outside.

He reaches for my hand. It's so tempting, but the rush of adrenaline is gone and the bridge's magic has faded. My step to the side of the walkway was meant to be subtle but comes off as blatantly obvious.

Sage pulls his hand back and sighs. "I wish I knew who hurt you."

"It wasn't intentional." I keep walking, hoping he won't notice how I've stiffened.

"If… if you ever want to talk about it, I'm here," Sage says.

I can't. I not ready. I'm not strong enough to talk about Robbie. Maybe I'll never be strong enough.

Sage waits for my answer. I simply nod.

I glance back at the Harbour Bridge. Somehow, being up so high, away from all of life's realities, made it easy to give in to temptation. Back on the ground, thoughts of Robbie rush back to haunt me.

Chapter
14

We're standing in front of a large sign that reads, "Welcome to the Royal Botanical Gardens. Please walk on the grass. We also invite you to smell the roses, hug the trees, talk to the birds, and picnic on the lawns."

The Australians are certainly more easy-going than folks back home. The signs in Ohio's metro parks are all of the "don't" variety: "Don't step off the trail, don't feed the wildlife, don't enter the water."

My self-imposed restrictions aren't so different, but it's refreshing to be in a land of "do's." Maybe I should try to be freer while I'm here.

"Are you ready?" Sage reaches for my hand but changes his gesture mid-motion and turns awkwardly toward the entrance. If I'm going to work at freeing myself, I might as well start now. I take his hand in mine.

"Are you sure? You don't have—"

"Let's go." I squeeze his warm palm gently as we step into the gardens.

Odd-shaped trees dot the grass, flowers bloom in clusters, and unusual plants grow all around us. Art decorates the gardens as well; all sorts of sculptures are placed strategically around the grounds. Sage leads me down a trail but pauses in front of a bronze goddess. Flower petals have been woven into a necklace and head wreath, while more petals and decorative leaves cover the base of the sculpture.

"Look at all the offerings. We should leave one, too." Sage heads to a nearby flowerbed. He searches the soil until he locates a fallen petal. Returning to the goddess, he places the petal on her outstretched hands.

"I thought you believed in the Buddha."

"I've found many of the Buddhist concepts... comforting," Sage says. "But I'm pretty open religiously."

I want to ask about the comforting comment, but something makes me think he's not ready to share more. "Open? How does that work?"

"Remember the first day we met, when I said I'm an explorer? Well, that goes for religions, too." He looks at the sky. "How can you know what you believe unless you explore each path?"

"I don't believe in anything," I admit.

"Makes sense. You're a runner, after all."

Sage had me pegged from that first conversation. He pulls a blanket from his backpack and spreads it on the ground. He reaches in his pack again and grabs a brown paper bag.

"We're going to have a picnic?" My stomach rumbles. The bridge climb took so long, we totally missed lunch. By the position of the sun, I would guess it's dinner time already.

"I figured we'd be starving by now, so I grabbed some food."

"When?" I'm still not used to someone being so thoughtful.

"While you were in the bathroom." He unpacks the contents. Two different cream-colored mushy things, pita sandwiches, and more pita bread. "Hope you like Mediterranean."

I've always been more of a meat and potatoes girl. I examine the mush. "What is it?"

"Hummus and baba ganoush." He gestures to the sandwiches. "I got some falafel, too."

I take a piece of pita, which I recognize, but I can't decide which mush is the safest one to try. "Your mom must be a health food nut."

"No, we ate pretty normal growing up." He lowers my hand to the hummus. "Try this one."

I dip my bread so only the top corner is covered before tentatively tasting it. Not bad. Not great, but not bad. "If you weren't raised vegetarian, how did you get into the healthy eating thing?"

Sage stops mid-bite then awkwardly swallows. "Let's just say, I had… motivation."

Motivation? What kind of answer is that? He's in excellent shape. Maybe he was an athlete at some point. I know they can have odd eating habits. Or maybe it was more ethical-related motivation. I could totally see Sage being a card-carrying member of PETA.

"What kind of—?"

"This must be one of the prettiest views in all of Sydney." Sage stares across the gardens at the view of the harbor and the Opera House.

His attempt to change the subject isn't lost on me, but having been there myself so many times, I'm not going to pry. "Definitely the best picnic view I've ever had. Is that why you chose the gardens?"

He glances at the sky, which is just starting to take on the pink hues of dusk. "Nope, it was just an added bonus. Hurry up so we're not late."

I finish my sandwich, which wasn't nearly as bad as I feared, then help Sage pack all our trash back into the brown bag. He takes my hand without hesitation this time, consults his map, and leads me to the left.

"Late for what?" Why all the mystery?

"You'll see." Sage stops underneath a grove of trees.

When I secluded myself in the dorms, I grew used to things being repetitive and predictable. Boring, but safe. Lately, I can't anticipate what's going to happen next. After arranging his blanket, Sage lies face-up and pats the empty space next to him.

"What are we doing? It looks like you're getting ready for a nap." I sit on the blanket, but Sage guides me down until we lay shoulder-to-shoulder.

Before I came to Australia, it had been six months since I lay next to a boy. Six lonely, lonely months. Not that the months before were much more bearable. Somehow, I've lain next to Sage twice since arriving.

I'm aware of everything. How his arm grazes me, the warmth of his leg pressed against mine, his gentle breaths on my cheek. "Are you comfortable?" he asks.

Comfortable is not how I'd describe it. My body's hypersensitive, and my mind's a mess. One half fights not to run away, and the other itches to get even closer.

"Look!" He points to the sky. A dark shape swoops out of the closest tree and glides through the air.

"Bats?" Another swoops down, then a third. Their huge black shadows contrast with the rosy-hued sky. Hundreds more hang upside down from the trees all around, releasing themselves one by one into the approaching night.

Sage nods, but these can't be normal fruit bats. They're enormous, far larger than the bats at the Cleveland Zoo. The bats fly away en masse as the sky darkens to lavender. Only one species fits the size and the location. "They must be flying foxes."

Sage takes his gaze off the bats for a moment and turns to me. "See, I knew you must have read at least one guidebook."

I shake my head. "I was a wildlife biology major when I was in school."

"Was?" he asks.

"I dropped out before coming here."

"Why?" Sage hesitates, as if speaking will break the spell and cause my barriers to come barreling back up.

Bats soar through the air. He couldn't have known *this* would be the perfect way to end our day in Sydney. I'm afraid to ruin the moment by bringing up ghosts from my past. "Let's just watch."

He turns back to the sky. A moment later, his fingers intertwine with mine. The warmth drives away the last of the memories, until only Sage, the world's largest bats, and the fragrant smells of the garden remain.

68

Chapter
15

By the time we get ready to leave, the sky has darkened and the bats have departed. So have all the other visitors. "Where did everyone go?"

"The park closes after the bat's performance. We'd better head out." Sage leads us along the deserted paths. With the sun gone, the night air takes on a slight chill. While it's probably still warm to most, I've always run colder than others. As we near the water, a breeze blows just enough to make me shiver.

Sage begins to wrap his arm around me, but he hesitates. His unspoken question becomes clear: *Is this okay?*

Instead of responding in words, I nestle closer to him. I'm not ready to admit that his touch is more than okay. It's freeing.

Not to mention confusing. I don't want to waste our trip thinking too much about Sage or Robbie. When we return to Susan's, I'll sort through my feelings.

Silently, we make our way back toward the Opera House. The city lights reflect off the harbor waters, illuminating the boats with their glow. The entire day has been so wonderful, I want to sigh in disappointment that it's come to an end. "We better head to the ferries before they stop for the night."

"Actually." Sage stops. "I was hoping to do one more thing, if that's okay with you. We can catch one of the late-night ferries."

"What do you want to do?"

"Watch that." Sage points to the Opera House.

Its white, sail-like top has transformed into a series of screens. While the building maintains its same shape, images project onto the sails. A conductor stands in front of a full orchestra. He waves his wand, and sound pours from giant speakers.

"Can we stay?" Sage places his palms together. "Please, please, please!"

How can I resist?

People crowd the lawn around the Opera House. Sage searches for a blanket-sized space then spreads his handy blanket out once more. As soon as I'm sitting, he wraps his arm around me again. I let myself relax into his side, my head resting on his shoulder, as music surrounds us.

"They're projecting the orchestra that's playing inside," he whispers.

"Do you like classical music?"

He shrugs. "It sounds pretty, but I have no idea who's playing or what song it is. I *love* the idea of watching anything on an actual building. Whoever thought of that was genius!"

The music does sound pretty. Slow and sad at first, then building to an energetic, vibrant end.

"I'll be right back. I want to grab something," Sage says.

Before I can ask where he is going, Sage has taken off. He joins a line for concessions, and the screens draw my attention back. A light show replaces the orchestra. Colorful shapes and lines move to the beat of the music.

Is this what going on a real date feels like? While Sage hasn't called it that, he's been extra attentive to my needs and free with his affection. I can't help but compare today to moments with Robbie, where everything centered on his needs. I love not having the burden of worry. To be free to just enjoy. To be taken care of, instead of always being the caretaker.

Guilt begins to rise, but just as I unzip my backpack for a piece of stationery, Sage sits down. "Just amazing how they put the images to the music so perfectly. Reminds me of that kid's show I used to watch when I was little. You know, the one with the broomsticks?"

I glance at Sage then zip the pocket. I want tonight to play out without interruptions, guilt, or obligation. "What do you have?"

He hands me a plastic glass filled with a red liquid. When I sniff, the contents become obvious. "Wine?"

"Their house red. I hope it's okay. Only one thing could top listening to music outside the Sydney Opera House."

"Oh yeah?"

"Drinking a glass of good wine, next to a beautiful girl, while listening to music outside the Opera House." He grins at me then holds his glass out.

I hesitate. "I'm not twenty-one. It's not like I've never had a drink, but I don't want to get you in trouble."

He smiles even wider. "You've been legal for nearly a year in Australia. Cheers!"

Sage holds his glass out, so I pick mine up and gently bump his before sipping the fragrant red. Sage moves behind me, and I rest against him. His heart thrums beneath my left cheek. Sage plays with a lock of my hair, wrapping it around his finger again and again. The music's intoxicating, and Sage's touch has an even bigger effect on me.

After finishing my wine, I'm warm, tingly, and sensitive to every one of Sage's touches. I cannot stop thinking about the way he kissed me atop the bridge... or how I responded.

Sage remains fixated on the music, the magical show, and the colored lights reflecting off the harbor waters. When the concert finally ends, he helps me up. "Best day ever!"

I only wish he had said, "Best date ever."

Chapter
16

When we finally make our way off the ferry, I glance in the direction of the water taxis. "Do you think they run this late?"

Sage grabs my hand and tugs in the other direction. "They stopped running two hours ago."

"What? You knew they closed so early?"

He turns to me, still holding my hand. "I checked with Susan yesterday. These little towns shut down after dark."

I pull away from him. "How are we going to get back?"

"I hope you're not mad, but I planned a surprise."

"Surprise? What about—"

"Susan? She gave us the weekend off. She isn't expecting us back until Monday." Sage begins to walk. "Besides, she helped me with the surprise."

He planned an entire weekend and didn't even bother telling me. I would have never agreed to stay with Sage for the weekend, which is probably why they didn't tell me. At least Susan insisted I pack clothes.

I should feel angry, but I'm so relieved our time isn't going to end. I'm not quite ready to return to my world of loneliness and purple envelopes.

As we leave the blocks of stores behind, the streetlights' dim glow fades until we're walking in darkness. Sage pulls a flashlight from the side pocket of his backpack. The strong glow lights the path in front of us, which winds toward the water. "Abby, I hope you aren't too mad. Seeing the Opera House at nighttime was one of the things on my list."

"Your list? What list?"

Sage quiets. We hike in silence for the next few minutes. "Don't you have a list of all the things you want to do and see in the world? Maybe not an actual paper list, but ideas that flow through your head?"

My whole world centered on Robbie for so long, I never took the time to think about my dreams.

"Really?"

He must have seen me shake my head. I would have been more careful if I knew the darkness wouldn't hide me.

"So coming here wasn't fulfilling some lifelong dream?"

"No. I just needed to leave. The destination wasn't important." I breathe—long and deep—three times. We are treading dangerous waters here. I don't want to sink.

"My little Wander." He runs his hand through my hair. "Wandering away from her past."

"Sage," I whisper.

Sage switches the serious for the whimsical. "I had a *wanderful* time exploring Sydney with you."

I can't help but giggle. "Feeling corny, are we?"

As we round the corner, the path leads to a grassy knoll overlooking the water. The tree cover is sparse here, allowing the moonlight to shine down on the little clearing. Immediately in front of us is a fire pit, already filled with logs and kindling. Sage searches through his backpack then strikes a match to the kindling. He slowly breathes into the sparks until they grow into dancing flames. As the firelight illuminates the clearing, a tent becomes visible in the distance.

"We're camping?" I have never camped before. My parents

were more comfortable in fancy four-star hotels. My friends went on a few camping trips in high school, but I always stayed behind with Robbie. Since Robbie couldn't camp, I chose not to.

He watches for my reaction. "Are you excited?"

"Surprised. How did you set this all up?"

"Susan lent me her tent and a few sleeping bags. She also drew a map of how to find this spot."

I settle onto a fallen tree, which serves as a bench along the fire pit. "I've never been camping before."

"Never?" Sage's leg brushes mine as he sits next to me.

I shake my head.

"Never ever? And camping isn't on your list?"

"We already talked about how I don't have a list." I'm not ready to get into the questions that are sure to follow. The moonlight shines upon the tiny waves that lap against the cliff. From this high up, it's difficult to see the water clearly, but the waves gently churn. "It's beautiful up here."

"Sure is." He traces one finger along my hairline, down my cheek, and under my chin. "Simply *wanderous*."

I sigh with disappointment when his finger leaves my skin. I want him to touch me more. At the same time, I want to run back to the safety of my isolation. "If you keep using that nickname, I'll have to come up with one of my own."

He grins. "Try your worst."

"Well, if I'm Wander, then you must be Roam. Roaming as far away as you can to avoid your future."

Sage wraps his arm around me. Between the heat of the fire and his body, the summer night's chill dissipates. "We make a fine team," he whispers in my ear. "Wander and Roam."

I try to ignore the tingle that runs from my ear down my neck. "It sounds like the type of song my grandparents listened to back in the day. An old sixties song."

Sage grabs a long, skinny log from the woodpile and pretends to strum it. "Don't wander away," he sings. "I want you to stay."

I find two long sticks and rhythmically pound them against a log.

"No matter where I roam," he calls, "you feel like home."

We sing and make silly jokes until the logs have burnt to ashes. The lower the flames grow, the more nervously I look at the tent. I wonder what Sage is expecting tonight.

"Are you ready to lie down? We have a busy day tomorrow." Sage picks up a bucket of dirt. Before he can dump it on the smoldering embers, I grab his arm.

"Sage, I'm not sure…" I glance at the tent. "I'm not quite ready to…"

"What?" His eyes widen after a moment. "Oh, I didn't mean for you to think… We can sleep on completely opposite sides, if you want."

"Maybe not that far away." I can't even meet his gaze.

I must be completely confusing him. Heck, I'm confusing myself. I want to run from his touch, but at the same time, I yearn for it. Tonight, I don't want to sleep alone, but I'm not quite ready for more.

"Can we snuggle?" I ask.

Sage dumps the dirt then leads me into the tent. "I am the biggest snuggle-monster."

He pulls our sleeping bags together, unzipping and re-zipping until they form a single bag. We climb into the cozy shell, my back to his front. Sage rests one hand on my belly and the other on my arm. His soft exhales blow onto my neck, sending tingles in their wake.

I drift into the warmest, safest sleep I have had. Not once does Robbie haunt my dreams.

Chapter
17

When I open my eyes, Sage is nowhere to be found. Maybe his absence is a blessing, because I have no idea how to treat him after yesterday. Groggily, I unzip the tent and stumble out into the already warm morning.

"Good morning, sleeping beauty." Sage hands me a tin cup full of steaming coffee. "Two sugars, no cream, if I remember right."

He actually took the time to memorize my coffee likes. To hide my smile, I raise the cup and sip. The hot liquid nearly scalds my mouth.

"Careful, I plan on using those later." He traces my lips with one finger. "Try not to burn them."

I stare down into the swirling blackness. The memory of his touch lingers on my bottom lip. Sage's bold words make me want to flee, but thoughts of yesterday stop me. For the first time in months, my loneliness disappeared for twenty-four straight hours. Instead of sitting around and pitying myself, focused entirely on the past, I took time to enjoy life in the present.

"Did you have fun yesterday?" Sage fiddles with a pan on top of the camp stove.

I can't remember the last time I had so much fun. "I... I did."

"You sound surprised."

"It's been a long time since..." I don't know how to finish. Thankfully, he's still cooking so I have space while I figure out how much I want to share. "Since I let myself enjoy life."

Something sizzles on the stove. He stirs the pan then sets down his spoon. "Abby, this is more serious than I thought."

"What do you mean?"

"Not allowing yourself to relish life is a tragedy." He resumes cooking. "I mean, each and every day should be cherished, but if that's too hard, at least give yourself today."

"What's special about today?"

"We have the entire day to ourselves. One whole day to focus on *enjoyment*." He winks.

While part of me is relieved the flirting will continue, I don't know how to respond. Luckily, I don't need to, because Sage sets a tin plate upon my lap. Thick slices of Susan's bread lie slathered in dark pink jam. Something resembling scrambled eggs rests next to the bread.

"Is this our jam?" I ask.

"Susan packed a jar for us."

I take a bite of the scrambled stuff. Ugh, definitely *not* eggs. I try to keep my face neutral, but my nose scrunches despite my efforts.

Sage laughs. "I made a tofu scramble. It's filled with all sorts of garden veggies and herbs."

"What makes it egg-colored?"

"A sprinkle of turmeric."

I pick out the veggies I can identify. A slice of zucchini, a spinach leaf.

"Try it. It's super rich in protein and nutrients, and you'll need the energy on our hike today."

"Our hike?" He must have the whole weekend planned. Since staying busy helped yesterday, I can't get too upset. If I could keep thoughts of Robbie at bay the entire weekend, that would be a first.

*M*aybe I will give myself today. An entire day, without the burdens and binds of my past, sounds so tempting.

"Do you mind if we visit the beaches today?" Sage balances his plate upon his knee while placing his hands together in a pleading motion. "Please, please, please."

"Sure." As I told him before, I planned nothing for this trip. I probably would've never even gone into downtown Sydney if it weren't for Sage's eagerness. "Do the beaches have something to do with your list?"

"Maybe." He looks toward the ocean. "The beaches around here are supposed to be some of the best in the world."

"If we're going to the beach, why did you mention hiking?"

Sage's eyes light up. "There's this trail that runs along the ocean. You can stop at each of the beaches along the way."

"So we're going beach-hopping?" I'm so glad Susan suggested I pack my suit.

"You can be the first to change. I'll clean up." Sage gathers the dishes then throws dirt on the smoldering coals.

Inside the tent, I dig my bikini out of the bottom of my backpack. I can't remember the last time I went swimming. Maybe my freshman year. My freshman year of high school, that is.

After changing, I pack what I'll need for the day then sit by the still-warm ashes of the fire.

"I'll just be a minute." Sage disappears inside the tent.

He has done everything for our trip: made the arrangements, prepared the meals, set up the campsite. I open the cooler and fix our lunches, but the five-minute lunch prep isn't nearly enough contribution. When Sage unzips the tent and steps back into the sunshine, I throw my arms around him. For a long, silent moment, I press myself to him, resting my forehead against his chest.

"What—?"

I raise one finger to his lips. "Thank you. For the camping, for the trip-planning, for everything."

"No thanks for the scrambled tofu?" He winks before moving out of my embrace. Before he leaves my side, though, he entwines my fingers in his. "Let's check out Bondi."

Hours later, our fingers are still connected. As we float on our backs in the buoyant Bondi waters, we never separate.

Sage pulls me closer until we tread the water, face-to-face. He kisses each salty drop off my forehead, my cheeks, my nose, and my lips. I finally untangle our fingers only to wrap my arm around his neck.

We're deep in the water, past the splashing kids and wading old people, far enough out that the mass of bodies fades away. I gently suck on his bottom lip while holding onto him even tighter.

We barely need to move to stay afloat. I'm not sure if that's due to the salinity of the water or the newfound buoyancy of my heart. All I know is I'm kissing Sage, he's touching me, and we're together in this wide-open sea.

"I understand," I whisper between kisses.

He gently tucks a tendril of hair behind my ear. "Understand?"

"The 'now.'" I brush his upper lip.

"We can wash away everything out here—the past and the future, problems and worries—so it's just you and me. I've always loved that about the ocean."

And then he's kissing me. *Really* kissing me. I cling to him as my last hesitations and doubts float away, until it's just Sage and I swimming in the never-ending waters.

When we finally break apart, I have no idea how many minutes, or hours, have passed. The lukewarm water only partially cools me. I'm not sure if it's the sun's relentless rays or Sage's endless touch that has created this fire within.

"Thank you," he whispers. "I get to cross off one more item."

"What?" Words and thoughts slowly return to me. "We haven't even started the hike yet."

"Making out with a beautiful girl in a beautiful ocean." He grins.

I can't tell if he's joking again or serious. "That's something you've always wanted to do?"

He brushes my lips once more.

"I would've been satisfied with 'swimming in the ocean.'"

"How long has it been since you've swum in the ocean?" Sage's fingers tease the soft, exposed skin around my waist.

"Never." I look toward the crowded beach, busy with families and sunbathers. "Beaches had too much sand and salt and stuff for my mother. As a kid, we would visit big cities like Toronto and New York. See the shows, eat at the fancy restaurants, shop in the high-end stores."

"Never?" His fingers still. "What about with friends? You must've gone on a spring break trip. Isn't that the senior ritual?"

"I never travelled with my high school."

"Not once? What about band trips or college campus visits?" Sage stares at me. He must realize something's off about my answers. I won't give him the opportunity to keep asking.

"I wasn't interested in extracurriculars." I begin to doggy-paddle back to the shore.

When I glance back, Sage is still treading water. He watches me. His eyebrows lift as if to ask, "What did I say?"

"What about that beach-hopping hike?" I call before swimming away from the questions, away from the answers, and even further from Sage.

Chapter
18

Sage was absolutely right. Everyone should experience the Bondi to Coogee hike at some point in their lives. Our walk up steep cliffs overlying the ocean, down to secluded beaches, then up again, leaves me winded.

Well, I can't actually tell if my breathlessness is due to the stunning scenery, the challenging hike, or Sage's persistent kisses. If I have to be honest, it's probably not the hike, as Sage stops me every few feet. He points out an orb-weaver's web, a lone wildflower, and ancient rock carvings. With each stop, he strokes my cheek, brushes back my hair, or caresses my lips.

As we come across the first beach, Sage spots surfers far out in the water. "Want to make a bet?"

"What kind of bet?"

"Who'll catch their wave?" He points to the brightly colored bodies dotting the ocean. "You win, you collect a favor. I win, the favor's mine."

"What kind of favor are you expecting?"

His smile spreads across his face. "If I told, that would take all the fun out of it. Are you in?"

"You'll rue the day you bet me." I turn my attention to the water. "You haven't discovered my competitive side."

"You? Competitive? I don't believe it." Sage leads us off the trail and down to the beach. He finds a spot in the warm sand, not too far from the water, and sits.

After settling next to him, I study the surfers. One who must be a newbie slips off his board before the first wave even hits. He's easy to eliminate from my prospect list. Two others catch the wave but seem a bit wobbly on their boards. "Purple Shorts" and "Orange Wetsuit" are also crossed off.

"Ready?" Sage takes my hand. He focuses more on me than on the boarders in the water. His thumb caresses my palm, and the gentle touches make it difficult to concentrate on the surfers.

"Stop, you're distracting me." I cannot remember the last time I had the freedom to let out my hidden rivalry. The heavy stuff has weighted down the last few years so much, I couldn't think of winning and competitions. But here—now—nothing seems more important than winning our bet.

After watching the surfers for ten more minutes, I have my pick. "Pink Board Shorts."

"Really?" Sage gapes at me. "My vote is with Brodie. I mean, 'Black Suit.'"

"You actually named your pick?" Both surfers swim deeper out into the water.

"Naming my surfer guy feels more... dignified."

I giggle. "That may be the first time 'dignified' and 'surfer' have been used in the same sentence."

A large wave begins to surge. I grab Sage's upper arm and squeeze. "Look!"

"Surf's up!" He teases me with his finger as he runs it down my leg to my toes. His gaze never leaves the water. "Come on Brodie!"

"Pinkie, Pinkie, Pinkie," I chant.

The wave crests, and sure enough, Pinkie and Brodie are the only ones riding it. Until Brodie falls off his board and disappears into the water.

"I win!" I jump up and dance around the sand in victory.

"I was really hoping for that favor." Sage draws me close. "How do you want to redeem it?"

I whisper in Sage's ear, "I think I'll save it. You never know when you're going to need a favor."

I place my hand in Sage's and turn back toward the trail.

The next beach lies deserted. Blue waves lap at the golden sand. After the crowded Bondi shore, this secluded patch calls to me. "Can we check this beach out?"

Sage leads the way down a steep stone staircase built right into the cliff. He disappears from my view. I follow his path and find myself underneath a rocky overhang, completely hidden from the trail.

"I would love to hang out for a few minutes." I glance around. The back half of the nook forms a half-cave, but the front is open to the ocean.

"We're definitely hanging out!" Sage grins. "This nook has all sorts of possibilities."

"Oh?" I can't help staring. He's so cute when he gets this enthusiastic.

He draws me close. The waves crash behind me. The sun angles into our hidden nook. Sage's hands rest on my back, warming me even more. He plays with the thin straps of my bikini. "You're missing the pretty view," he whispers before spinning me around. Sage pulls me taut against his body, and we watch the ebb and flow of the waves. At least, I try to watch the water, but Sage's closeness is so distracting, I cannot focus.

His arms encircle me, and his hands rest on the sensitive skin of my belly. His warm breath caresses the back of my neck with each exhalation. He holds me so close, I can't move or touch him back. I can only feel.

"I want..." I breathe.

"Tell me what you want." His breath tickles my ear.

I can barely breathe, let alone talk. Sage pulls me even closer. The word builds inside. I focus on the waves, on the cool sand underneath my feet, on the tiny sailboat that floats across the distant horizon.

One caress of his lips against my neck is my downfall. A single word slips out, released to the world. "You."

Sage releases me immediately. My disappointment's momentary, though, for he spins me around again then lowers his lips to mine. Throughout his endless caresses and kisses, not once do I feel the need to open my backpack for stationery.

Chapter
19

I lead the way along the next portion of the trail. After my unplanned disclosure, which surprised even me, I can barely look at Sage. He accepts my need for space and strolls a few yards behind me.

I want... My cheeks warm at the memory. If Sage notices their flush, maybe—hopefully—he'll attribute it to the hot Australian sun. I have never had that yearning with anyone. Not through high school. Not in my first year of college. Not even with Robbie.

Robbie. I have barely thought about Robbie. He didn't invade my thoughts in Sydney, and I certainly wasn't thinking of him on that deserted beach. Surprisingly, I haven't written one letter this weekend. Up to now, I don't think a single day has passed that I haven't folded my thoughts, my wishes, my dreams, into one of Robbie's special purple envelopes. While a small part of me cheers, *This is how healing works*, another part has no desire to forget.

"Best view forevermore," Sage calls. "Lucky guys."

I've been so lost in my thoughts, I haven't even paid attention to our surroundings. When I look up, expecting more coast and wildflowers and interesting cliff formations, the actuality of what looms in front of us freezes me.

I stare. I just stand along that terribly cruel trail and stare. I try to move, to think, but my body freezes, and my mind numbs. Row after row after row of gravestones rise out of the ground to the right of the trail. Hundreds, no, thousands of graves mock me.

Silently, I hike off the trail and through the old metal gates. A sign, preserved with time, reads, *Waverly Cemetery*. Somehow, I'm walking among the graves. While some of the tombstones are the modern kind, flat slabs of marble resting on the ground, the majority feature elaborate stone statues and carvings rising high above my head.

I shouldn't be here.

I walk faster, read dozens of names as I pass by. No matter how fast I walk, I cannot escape the reminders. Finally, I break into a run then sigh as the names morph into a long, etched blur.

Until two interlocked hearts, engraved into one statue's marble, catch my eye. *Our* symbol. I stop to glance at the stone, which is a terrible mistake, for my pause is long enough to read the first name. *Robert. His* name.

While the centuries are different, the continents are different, the combination of *that* symbol and *that* name are my undoing. I collapse to the manicured grass, lie across the sun-warmed stone, and sob. Long, painful wails combine with raspy gasps for air. Liquid grief pours down, covering my face, sliding down my neck, soaking my shirt.

Muted footsteps pound the cement path. Hands hold my heaving, aching body. A voice says, "Abby, oh Abby."

None of it helps. I couldn't care less about Sage's soothing words, his loving hands, or his comforting body. I tried to run. But my grief has finally caught up with me, even though I'm half the world away. I guess sorrow is one of those inescapable things.

So I lie across the cool marble and whisper my apologies. Even though it's the wrong Robert, I imagine my words carving a path straight through the earth. Waverly Cemetery, Sydney, New South Wales, Australia to Holy Souls Burial Ground, Cleveland, Ohio, United States.

When I've cried every drop out, when my body cannot heave a single more time, I finally stand. Sage sits quietly upon a bench, far enough away to give me privacy but near enough that I can easily spot him. He watches, still and silent, as I approach.

"I'm sorry," he mumbles. "I didn't know."

"H-how would you?" My throat's raw. "I don't talk about my past."

"Ever?" Sage searches through his backpack until he finds a water bottle.

I take the bottle that Sage offers. The cool liquid soothes the parchedness, but my abused voice still sounds raspy. "S-since he, you know, d-d…"

"Died?" Sage whispers.

All I can do is nod. *Since Robbie died.* After all these months, all these years of knowing and expecting the inevitable, why can't I speak the words?

"That's what you've been running from?" Sage studies me, but he doesn't try to touch me, thankfully. I don't know if I could bear his affection in front of the other Robert's grave.

"I-it happened last summer. I shut down. We were together for nearly five years, since my sophomore year of high school, and then he was just gone."

Sage studies his shoes, as if he's searching for the right thing to say. "An accident?"

I take a few moments to gather my thoughts. I've never told anyone the story, not the complete one, anyway. "Can we talk somewhere else? Away from—"

Sage jumps up. "Absolutely."

As we head to the next beach, visible on the horizon, I think of where to begin. "I met Robbie in my algebra class, freshman year."

"Was he a freshman, too?" Sage studies me, checking that his question was okay.

"He was a sophomore. I'm hopeless at math, and he volunteered as a tutor. We met twice a week for tutoring sessions after school." The memory of a younger Robbie, more boy than man, floods me. "We goofed around and told jokes and got a little math done."

Sage sits along a flat section of rock, worn smooth by weather.

I settle next to him but leave a gap between us.

"I didn't see him at all the first summer, and I missed him." Missed him from the perspective of a young teen, who had no idea what truly missing someone really meant. "When he saw me, the first day of my sophomore year, he asked me out. He said his summer was lonely without me."

Sage waits, watches, and does not try to touch me.

"When we figured out we *really* liked one another, he told me about his kidney disease." I glance at Sage, who clenches his fists so tightly he must be carving nail marks into his palms. "That long ago, it didn't seem like a big deal. Robbie needed to be on some medicines, and he was really careful about his diet, but he seemed healthy enough." My words pour out. Once you turn the faucet on, the water just wants to flow and flow and flow. "Everyone thinks they're invincible at that age, right?"

"Invincible, yeah, I guess." Sage stares out at the ocean.

"But the following year, Robbie's senior year, his symptoms grew worse. His kidneys slowly shut down, and he was able to do less and less. Finally, he went into renal failure."

"He passed that long ago?" Sage asks in a quiet voice.

"He spent the next eighteen months on the transplant list. During my senior year, I spent as much time at the hospital as I did at school. Robbie was on dialysis three days per week, four hours per day."

"You went with him?" Sage sounds surprised.

"Of course. I spent every possible minute with him."

"No spring break, no extracurriculars, no wonder." Sage's eyes widen. "You sacrificed your high school years for him, didn't you?"

"Of course, he was my... *everything*." I run my hand along the warm stone. "I wanted to switch schools, attend the local community college, but my father insisted I attend the university I'd been accepted into."

"You would've given up—?"

"I should've been there for his last year." Tears begin to fall once more, although I have no idea where my body summoned up more liquid. "I should have been there."

"Shh." Sage embraces me, and I yearn so badly for comfort, I accept his warm, strong hug. "You couldn't have known."

"He was on the transplant list." I sniffle. "When they found a match, we all had so much hope."

"What happened?" Sage holds me even tighter.

"After a few months, his body rejected the kidneys then shut down, one part at a time. Within the week, he…"

The tears return. Tears of guilt for not being there that first year of college, tears of grief for remembering those beautiful, awful times, and tears of *relief*. I'm finally able to talk about Robbie.

Maybe, if I'm ready to talk about our relationship, I'm also ready to say my goodbyes.

I grab my backpack, sling it back over my left shoulder, and step onto the trail. Not heading forward, but backward. Back to Waverly Cemetery, back to the tombstones that haunt me, back to what I've spent the past six months running from.

"Where are you going?" Sage calls as I force myself to take one cautious footstep after another.

"Wait here. I need to be alone for a while." Each step takes me closer to what I dread, what I've hidden from, what I need to do.

Finally, the metal gates appear. I stare at the endless rows of graves. A single flower rests in a weighted vase upon a nearby stone. Its petals flutter in the salty breeze.

I look for the two interlocking hearts, the familiar name etched in stone. Earlier, my flight through the cemetery had been so frantic that retracing my steps is hard. But after forty-five minutes of searching—looking at each name, reading each date, honoring each memory—I find the heart-carved stone.

I open my backpack, pull out my notebook, and free my pen from the wire spiral. *How can I possibly begin? How do I say goodbye?* While I'll never be fully ready, this farewell needs to happen. I cannot live my entire life as a shell. Robbie would want me to have closure.

I hold pen to paper, remember our love, our time together, us, and write.

Wander & Roam

Dear Robbie,

You'll never imagine how I spent the day, crying in an Australian cemetery over someone else's grave. Those two interlocking hearts were my undoing. Did I ever tell you how your mother let me choose the symbol to be etched onto your gravestone? I think she felt it would bring me closure. I agonized over my choice, before settling on the two hearts. Just like we used to draw in each other's notebooks. Just like we carved in that tree in the Cuyahoga Metropark.

My mother said it was a sign for an old married couple who planned on being buried together, but I didn't care. I wanted you to feel my love for eternity.

But I cannot hold onto this love forever. I'm sinking, Robbie. The grief, the loss—of you, of us—carries me down. I love you, I will always love you, but I remember your last words, "Live, for me."

You will always be my first love. While I'll never forget your memory, it's time for me to start living again. You would want that. The old, laughing, goofy Abby, rather than this shell of an Abby that I've become. Goodbye, Robbie Williams.

XXXOOO

Abby

As tears splatter the paper, I fold it then place it in one of the small purple envelopes. I begin to stick it into my backpack with the dozens of other letters that crowd my front pocket but look back at the tombstone. After a long pause, I place the envelope into a crevice along the top of the marble. Slowly, I insert the other envelopes wherever they fit, until purple lines the carving.

Hopefully, the other Robert, *1848-1898,* will not mind.

I make my way back to the trail. Tears continue to trickle when I finally find Sage. "Ready to finish our hike?"

"Are you okay?" He wipes a droplet from my cheek.

What does "okay" even mean?

Holding onto Robbie for so long has been destructive. I haven't just lost my beloved; instead, I've screwed up my schooling, ruined

90

my friendships, and angered my family. By refusing to let go, I nearly lost myself.

My aboveground tomb looked different from Robbie's, but the end result was pretty much the same. If I'm ever going to be *okay*, I need to move on.

We continue the last stretch to Coogee in silence. The sun has just begun to sink, and pinks and oranges illuminate the ocean. The smell of the ocean scents the air as I wipe the last salt-tinged tears from my face.

When the trail ends, we find the bus stop and ride silently back to the ferry landing. The last ferry moves through purple-hued skies and lavender waters. Finally, we reach our campsite. Sage builds a fire. As its warm glow lights up the night, I open up my backpack then pull out the hundreds of unused envelopes that remain. One by one, I fling the purple rectangles into the blaze. Each causes the fire to surge.

Sage sits right next to me, despite the length of the log. "Are you sure?"

"Robbie gave me the envelopes when I left for college." I throw another one into the fire. "So that each time he saw a purple envelope, he would know immediately that it was 'precious.'"

"You wrote to him the old-fashioned way?"

"Every day." I remember my college ritual, sitting in my dorm with pen, paper, and purple envelope. "Sometimes, on hard days, more than once."

"Why—?"

"He was worth the effort. I mean, we talked on the phone, texted, and video chatted, too, but taking the time to write showed how much I cared." The blaze intensifies as another envelope hits the flames.

"You never stopped writing."

"The ritual—writing to Robbie, folding my letter, sealing the purple envelope—brought me comfort. Sometimes, it was the only thing that did." I hold the last envelope in my hands. *Goodbye, Robbie.* I prepare to throw it.

"Don't!" Sage grabs it. "Sorry, I have an idea for the last one. Something we can do back at the farm."

"I just want to forget. I've spent too much time grieving." I've written my daily letters, month after month, as if Robbie was on a long trip instead of buried in the ground. I've avoided cemeteries and all talk of death, so I could pretend he wasn't really gone. I cannot bear any more sadness.

If I don't find a way to move on, *I'm* not going to make it.

He squeezes my hand. "Today's been overwhelming. Why don't you sleep on it?"

The inky blackness surrounds us, with only small licks of fire lighting our campsite. Today *has* been overwhelming. Between our romantic morning swim, the exhausting hike, and my cemetery meltdown, I've been riding an emotional rollercoaster. I'm never going to fall asleep.

And if I do, I'm terrified that memories of Robbie will haunt my dreams.

Sage's warm leg presses against me. His arm, all muscles and tone, rubs against the softness of mine. His scent—salt-kissed sunshine and ocean water—surrounds me. I can't help but remember the highs of that morning. Only ten hours earlier, I had been so happy. I want, no, *need*, to replicate those moments. I need to forget.

"Abby?" Sage watches me carefully.

"Make me forget, Sage." I lay my head against his shoulder.

Sage leans down, zips the envelope into his backpack's pocket, then wraps his arm around me. "I'm not sure this is the best time."

"Please!" I hold his face close, rest my forehead upon his, and kiss the bridge of his nose. "Remember my words earlier? I meant them."

Sage inhales suddenly. When I lean back, his eyes darken. He stares at me with desire, longing, and... something else. Hesitation?

"You're worried it's too soon." I kiss his chin, his cheeks, and as he closes his eyes, each eyelid. "But you won't be taking advantage of me."

He sighs as I nip at his lower lip.

"You'd be helping me." I brush my lips against his. "I want to move on."

He grabs my shoulders and presses me to him. He runs his

hands down each arm then up again. "You're sure?"

"I'm sure," I whisper into his ear before nibbling on his lobe.

Sage's resolve melts with my teases. Breaking away, he rests his forehead against mine. "If you change your mind, just let me know."

I nod my understanding, but I've already decided. I need Sage's closeness, comfort, and caring. I need to be whole again, rather than this withered up version of myself.

Sage brushes his lips against the soft skin of my eyelids. His lips trace the trails of dried tears from my eyes to my cheeks then continue lower until they reach my neck. The whisper-soft brushes of his lips tease me until I press myself even closer to him. We merge together as best we can on the rough, bark-covered log.

"Can we move into the tent?" I stand, pull Sage up, and wait as he fiddles with the zipper. He gestures for me to crawl inside then enters after me.

"Oops, wait." He exits then throws a bucket of dirt onto the flames. The fire flickers out, and darkness surrounds me. Moments later, Sage reenters, zips up the tent, then turns to me. In the moments he was gone, my brazenness has faded into shyness. I hug him and savor the warmth of holding another so close. *It has been so long.*

He pulls me on his lap then resumes his slow exploration. I place my hands upon his chest. Through the thin fabric of his T-shirt, his heart thumps. Normally at first, but as my thumb circles his heart, faster and faster.

My heart speeds as well.

In the black of the night, in the isolation of our campsite, in the comfort of Sage's arms, I lose myself to him. Everything fades away but the two of us. Nobody else and nothing else matters. The peace that brings is nothing less than ecstasy.

Chapter
20

wake, safe in Sage's arms, as the sun warms the tent with its first rays. The temptation to remain snuggled close overpowers me. Our little tent shuts out the world, its thin canvas walls a barrier against memories, worries, real life.

Sage opens his eyes, a smile already forming on his face. "Morning."

The glow of sunlight streams through the leaf-green tent walls, painting Sage in nature's colors. I nestle closer and tuck my head against his shoulder. "I don't want to leave."

"Me either." He wraps both arms around me, pulling me closer.

Leaning my head back, I kiss the underside of his chin. His prickly, unshaven hairs tickle my lips. "Thank you."

"For what?" Sage holds me quietly.

"Helping me move on." I trail my fingers down his chest. "I don't know how much longer I could have survived."

"What do you mean?" His body stiffens.

"Losing someone I loved ripped a part of... *me* out. I spent six months feeling like I was drowning."

"Drowning?" His voice quiets.

"In my grief. For months, I never saw the surface—until, this weekend." I weave my fingers between his and gently raise them to my lips. "You gave me hope."

Sage doesn't say a word. I brush my lips against his knuckles, but he abruptly moves his hand out of my reach. "Susan will be waiting," he says. He jumps up, grabs his backpack, and abruptly exits. I'm left to wonder about what happened. *Disappointment over leaving or the awkwardness of the morning after?* I can't help but hope it's the first.

I slowly pull fresh clothes on, brush my hair for an extra-long time, and linger while tying my shoes. Last night, this tent served as a refuge from my grief and sadness. *What if it all comes rushing back as soon as I set foot outside?*

"Abby," Sage calls. "We need to hurry. The next water taxi leaves in a half-hour."

When I unzip the tent, he's all business. He has torn the camp down, with the exception of the tent I'm sitting in; the gear's carefully packed and piled; and the tent bag waits. I head to the tree line to brush my teeth, using my water bottle to wet the travel-sized toothbrush and rinse. By the time I finish, the tent's completely disassembled and packed.

Sage attaches it to the bottom of his enormous backpack. "Ready?"

No. I want to shake my head, shout my protests, and dig my heels into our little sanctuary. This weekend has been transforming. For months and months, I carried the weight of Robbie with me everywhere I went. Until now.

I'm finally free. I left that stiflingly heavy backpack of memories in the cemetery yesterday. I want to revel in my newfound freedom, enjoy life again. Spend more time with Sage.

"Come on." He's already walking toward the path. I grab my backpack, throw my dental supplies back in, and follow him.

Within five minutes of reaching Susan's dock, the breakfast bell tolls.

"I've missed Susan's cooking." He heads toward the dining table. "Might as well drop off her camping gear before bringing my pack back."

And then he's gone.

I wait in the yurt for as long as I can. While we never spoke of our expectations, Sage's obvious brush-off hurts me. I initiated everything that happened last night, though. I cannot blame Sage. It wasn't as if he seduced me with whispered promises.

I thought our connection was real.

I wouldn't even know what "real" feels like, with my inexperience. I can't help worrying I scared Sage off with my complete openness about the mess of my life since Robbie died. No one would want to get involved with that kind of dysfunction.

When I can't wait any longer, I head down to the dining area. Surprisingly, Susan still sits at the table, nursing little Zachary. She's usually not here so late.

"I'm sorry I'm so late. Don't worry. I'll still put in my five hours today."

"I'm not worried." She runs her fingers through Zachary's fine blond hair. "I imagine you were tired after your long weekend."

"Something like that." I pile a plate with fresh fruit, homemade granola bars, and cold pancakes.

"What did you think of Sydney?" She places the baby upright and pats him gently upon the back.

Sydney. I don't want to remember lying on the blanket watching the bats lift off nor the amazing kiss atop the Harbour Bridge. "Um." I cannot meet her eyes. "What a beautiful city."

"Abby, did something happen? Between you and Sage?" Susan glances at his still-empty seat. "I know it's none of my business, but if you need someone to talk with…"

"I'm fine. We're fine." I eat my remaining pancake in two large bites then wrap the granola bars in a napkin. "I just overdid it. Trying to fit the whole tourist experience into one weekend was pretty exhausting." I grab the granola bars and head off to the gardens. I remember my friends' sighs of annoyance whenever I tried to share my worst fears about Robbie's illness. When you're young, the last thing people want is to be reminded they're vulnerable to disease and accidents, too.

Once in the gardens, I'm completely alone. I settle among the bed of garden greens and pick a selection of salad greens: arugula, red leaf lettuce, and tender baby spinach leaves. When my bag is full, I move to the potatoes.

The repetitive work of digging up the red-skinned potatoes, shaking off the excess soil, and smoothing the ground is freeing. Here in the gardens, I can lose myself in my work and forget about all of life's outside stressors. Sage was right. Focusing on the present is freeing.

The thought of the present brings the hurt of Sage's absence back full force. *After all we shared this weekend, how could he avoid me?*

Chapter
21

After an entire day passes without any contact, I'm fed up. Sage must have stayed out until I fell asleep. I heard him rustling in the middle of the night, but by morning, he's already gone.

I need to confront him. I'm too fragile to deal with this hot-and-cold crap. The only problem with questioning him is finding him. In the last twenty-four hours, he's become an expert on disappearing.

The breakfast bells rings much earlier than normal. I throw on clothes and head down the trail. Since I probably won't even see Sage, I don't bother taking time to look cute. It's not as if he'll even notice me.

What changed?

Maybe this day-after brush off is normal. I wouldn't know, given that I've always been loyal to Robbie. I haven't been with anyone else, not in high school, not in college. Sage could think I was just a casual hook-up, but it's not likely with everything I shared.

When I reach the tables, he's actually sitting at one. He eats his breakfast without even looking up or saying hello. I fix my plate then pause in the gap between the tables. I could plop myself right next to him, making it impossible to avoid me or mimic his cold-shoulder routine and sit at the empty table. I've never been a confrontational person, and this mess I'm in is *so* personal. I'm afraid of losing control when we finally talk, but don't want to break down in front of Susan. She should be back any minute to collect the dishes.

I place my plate at the opposing table, so we're sitting back to back. Perfect. We can't see each other, so we don't have to talk to one another. *But if it's so perfect, why am I so upset?*

My lip starts to wobble, and tears well in my eyes. I quickly bite my lip, blinking back tears before they can fall. I force myself to take a bite of the oatmeal. I can barely swallow the thick, congealed mass.

"Well, don't you both look happy as can be?" Susan walks into the dining area, holding a fussy Zachary in her arms.

I stare into my bowl, mortified that Susan has probably guessed *why* we're not talking. Sage doesn't respond, either.

"I need a favor. A big one, given how friendly you're being to each other." Susan soothes Zachary as his fussing increases. "The poor little guy's running a temperature."

"Do you need some medicine? I could take the water taxi to town," Sage says.

"I wish it were only an errand trip." Susan sighs. "The farmer's market opens today. The money I make at the market funds the farm for the year."

"The produce won't last until next week." Sage stands and clears his dishes.

"Exactly." Susan gently rocks back and forth, and Zachary's cries soften into sleepy whimpers. "Can you and Abby handle it?"

Susan has so many responsibilities between raising a child and running a farm completely by herself. I would be happy to help her. "Of course—"

Sage cuts me off. "I think I can handle this on my own."

"No, it's a two-person job. I usually have a friend from town join me." Susan gives him a sharp stare. "Even with having breakfast early, we're already running late."

"You really can't handle spending one day with me?" My voice is so low, I'm not sure if he even hears me.

Sage's voice softens. "Abby, it's not that. I just thought—"

"The two of you can work out your differences once the produce is unloaded, but you really need to hurry." Susan quickly shares information about the market. "My friend will be waiting with his truck when you get to the dock."

For the next half-hour, we lug boxes of packed produce down the steep trail. It's an exhausting job since wheeled carts don't work on the rocky path. When the water taxi arrives, I help load the boxes in. Thankfully, nothing falls in the bay, which isn't an easy task given the boat's swaying.

We're so busy hauling and loading that we couldn't stop to chat even if we wanted to. But as the taxi takes off through the water, minute after minute silently passes. Sage chooses to stand at the bow, as far from my bench as he can possibly get on this tiny motorboat. My fists clench tighter and tighter as the dock approaches. At the very least, he owes me some answers. Maybe this awkward trip is a blessing. While we're manning the booth, he'll be trapped for six straight hours, unable to hide from me.

Now, I just need to figure out what to say.

The taxi docks one town down from where we caught the ferry. My taut muscles loosen. At least we won't have to walk through a place so ripe with memories.

A tall, heavyset man pulls his pickup truck to the edge of the dock when he sees the boat arrive. "Let's load it up! The market will open soon."

We lug each box of produce to the truck and slide it into the open back. The work goes quickly with all three of us helping. Before the man closes up the pickup, Sage hops into the back. "I'll ride back here."

I head to the passenger side. While we would have been cramped, the seat's long enough for three people. I can't help feeling snubbed. Again.

"My name's Lonnie." The man jumps into the front seat then holds out his hand. "Sorry, I should've introduced myself sooner."

"No worries. I know we're in a hurry." The waterside disappears as the truck weaves through the little town.

"You'll have an easier trip back," he says. "Usually, you sell out of most stuff, so you're just hauling empties home."

"Are you staying for the entire market?"

"Nope. I'll help you unload, then I need to bring Susan some supplies." He pulls onto a crowded street. Trucks line the side, and tables rest on the inside of the town square. "She said the two of you might need some time and space. Something about a lover's spat?"

My cheeks warm. This is a set-up to get Sage and me together to talk. It isn't even Susan's business. But I can't stay angry with her. She must have had good intentions.

"Come on." Lonnie parks and hops out. "Let's set up."

We settle into a routine. Sage carries the boxes of produce over, while I arrange it on the tables. We work in harmony together, probably because the set-up requires no communication from either of us. Within the half-hour, the truck's completely unloaded, and the tables brim with fresh produce.

"See you this afternoon." Lonnie waves before driving away.

I arrange each of the pricing signs that Susan packed. They're cute, with hand-drawn images of each type of produce. At the same time, Sage tests Susan's scale and sets out plastic bags along the tables. We're surprisingly efficient given we still haven't spoken a word to one other.

"Do you want to weigh the produce or take the money?" I finally ask.

"I'll weigh," he says.

With nothing more to do, we sit on folding camp chairs and wait for our first customers to arrive. The market opens in five minutes.

I break the silence. "Why are you ignoring me? Did I do something wrong?"

He studies the sidewalk so carefully, he could be counting ants. "I don't know if this is the best time to—"

"Well, you constantly disappear. This might be my *only* chance to get answers." I twist a rubber band around my finger. If I look at him, I'll never be brave enough to continue. "Are you going to answer me? What did I do?" **101**

"No, Abby. It's not you—"

"What am I supposed to think? I know I'm messed up, and I'm so sorry you had to witness *how* messed up on our hike, but..." *I don't know what else to say. How many times has he caught me crying or writing letters to my dead boyfriend?* Heck, I wouldn't even want to date me.

"I think you're brave." He lifts my chin until our eyes meet. "Brave and selfless. You give up so much of yourself for those you care about."

"What?" This entire time I assumed he saw me as the crazy girl who talks to dead guys.

"Look how you sat with Robbie for hours when he was in treatment, and how you wrote him letters every day." Sage strokes my cheek. "Most men would jump to have a girlfriend who was so loyal."

He thinks I'm brave, selfless, and loyal? "Why—?"

"Excuse me." A woman carrying a wicker basket approaches our table. "How much is the Swiss chard?"

"Um, let me check." I reluctantly leave Sage's side to find the fallen sign.

The next few hours are a whirlwind of activity. The booth remains packed with people filling bags and baskets with our produce. As soon as the crowd thins, we hurry to restock. Inevitably, another surge happens as soon as we fill our tables.

We fall into a steady routine. Weigh, accept payment, and restock. Repeat again and again and again. I'm dying to ask him about his kind words. *Does he really think I'm all of those positive things? Then why has he given me the cold shoulder for the last two days?* I simply don't have time to ask him anything, though.

In the late afternoon, most of the produce has sold. A small basket of potatoes, a few bruised tomatoes, and some wilted lettuce remain on the table. The farmers around us have sold out, too, and are packing away their supplies.

"Why are you ignoring me?" I finally ask.

He sighs. "I'm sorry. I didn't mean to flip the hot-cold switch on you."

That's exactly what he did. After weeks of the flirtatious, overly friendly Sage I knew, this new withdrawn, disengaged version of Sage is a stranger to me.

"Don't I deserve an explanation?" I ask.

"It's me, Abby." He grabs his hair in frustration. "I realized I'm not good for you."

Finally, Sage is ready to share an explanation of his aloofness. Just as I'm about to ask him more, Lonnie pulls up.

"Ready to head back, kids?" He pulls down the back of his pickup truck.

In complete silence, we load up the remains of the veggies and pack the empty boxes together. Sage climbs in the back once again, and I walk to the front. Lonnie chats the entire ride to the docks, but I stare quietly out the window at the little town.

When we board the water taxi, Sage resumes his stance by the bow. I thought we'd be able to resolve this awkwardness, but I really don't know anything more. I wonder why he thinks he isn't good for me. *Why does he think* he's *the problem?*

Chapter
22

After a week of awkward glances, forced smiles, and too much distance, I cannot bear it. I searched for release through the physically intensive farm work, but with every bed in the garden weeded, each ripe vegetable harvested and stored, garden tools washed and even polished, physical exertion isn't working.

Since nothing on this farm needs doing, I decide to walk. Without any planning or conscious thought, I find myself on the path up the cliff. When I reach the spot that overlooks the bay, I sink down on the soft grass. The white sails against blue waters don't distract me from this spot's first memory. Our first kiss, so spontaneous after Sage's lesson on being in the moment.

For the longest time, Robbie was my everything. My best friend, my confidante, my love, my soul mate. Truthfully, he was all of these and more. Everyone talks about true love, but nobody warns of the dangers of such an all-encompassing romance. When Robbie died, I forgot how to live.

For a few short weeks, Sage brought me back from my prison of the non-living. He full-on resurrected me. Rejoining the world was like watching an old movie that starts off black-and-white and ends in full Technicolor. Only between his cold shoulder and the loneliness of this farm, the grays have started to seep back in again.

I watch the blue sky and the bluer water until they blur. One by one, tears well over and run down my cheeks. When one droplet weaves its way to my lips, the tinge of salt brings back another memory, Sage's salty ocean kisses.

For the second Sunday in a row, I curl up on the ground and weep. I have no idea how long I cry. I need the release, though.

"Abby?" Sage's soft voice calls. His feet crunch against the forest debris, and his clothes rustle as he settles next to me.

I try to regain control, but my crying has gotten to the place where it overpowers me. How completely and utterly mortifying.

"I wish there was something I could do to ease your pain," he whispers. Something rustles—his backpack, I think. He presses a crisp rectangle into my hands. I would know that object anywhere. The smooth linen texture of fine paper. The slight hint of glue. I wipe away the tears with my arm as I open my eyes.

The last purple envelope.

"I just remembered I promised to do something special with this one, something to help you mourn." Sage rubs my back. I hate myself for it, but I lean into his touch.

He thinks I'm mourning Robbie. How can I tell him that I'm not mourning over what's gone? Instead, I'm crying over what will never be. For a few brief days, I allowed myself to hope... to dream... to imagine.

Only my musings centered entirely on Sage.

For months, I clung to the fading memory of Robbie. Despite all the thousands of pointless things they teach throughout high school and college, no one offers classes on how to mourn properly. Probably a skill few young adults need, I imagine.

Something changed in the cemetery. Grief's heavy, a stone-filled, sorrow-ridden backpack. When I tore away the straps of my burden of misery and abandoned it on that gravestone, the release was undeniable.

The world's prettiest view, for all perpetuity. Robbie would have liked that.

"The Japanese have a ritual to work through their grieving," Sage says. "Would you like to see if it helps?"

I refuse to embarrass myself by sharing what these tears were actually about, so I just nod.

He helps me to my feet then takes back the envelope. "I need a few hours to prepare. Meet me at the dock tonight for sunset."

Fifteen minutes after the dinner bell rings, I finally make my way to the covered eating area. A stoneware container holds a steaming soup, but only one bowl rests next to it.

Susan follows my gaze to the remaining bowl. "Sage already took his portion. He said he was too busy to join you."

Sage has been too busy to come to dinner all week. I've almost grown used to eating alone again. Almost, but not really.

Susan lowers her hand to mine. "I was wondering if you'd prefer to join me for dinner." When I hesitate, she adds, "I wouldn't mind the company. Zachary's not a great conversationalist."

"That sounds nice." I pick up the stoneware and walk behind her down the trail. As warmth spreads from the stone to my hands, I think about the irony of my situation. For months, I secluded myself. But now that I've cut the bonds of my isolation, I crave contact.

"I hope it's not too warm a night for soup. It's the height of harvest, so my kitchen's overflowing with veggies," Susan says.

"Soup actually sounds good." It smells good, too. I can't pick out all the different vegetables but recognize the pungent odor of garlic. "I still haven't gotten used to the idea of summer in December."

"You probably have a more traditional Christmas where you're from, huh?" Susan glances back, which gives Zachary a better view of me. He coos in my direction.

"If you count real snow most Christmas mornings as traditional." This will be the first time I'm away for the holiday.

"I would love to see that. The holiday lights against the snow. Santa in a sleigh instead of on a surfboard."

"Are... are you going to visit any family over the holidays?" If

I'm lonely after this past week, I can't imagine how she deals with the isolation.

"This little guy's the only family I have left," she says quietly. "My parents have both passed on."

I tickle Zachary's toes when I'm close enough to reach them. His laughter peals through the quiet evening.

"What happened to his father?" As soon as the question exits my mouth, I freeze in embarrassment. I should know better than anyone how painful inquiries about the past can be.

Susan pauses at her front door. "Some people aren't ready for life's responsibilities." Without further explanation, she turns the knob and gestures for me to enter. Susan's kitchen is dotted with signs of tonight's soup. A compost bucket teems with vegetable scraps, a stainless steel stockpot still rests on the cold burner, and chopped bits of carrots and greens dot a large cutting board.

"Excuse me while I change Zachary's nappy." Susan frees him from the sling. "I'll join you as soon as I'm done."

I set the soup on the wooden table. Her kitchen looks exactly as it did the last time I was here, on jam-making night. Only it's so much emptier without Sage's laughing, joking presence.

We didn't just convert the raspberry crop into jam that night. We transformed our fragile acquaintance into the sticky binds of attraction and friendship. Watching the berries solidify into a thick, sweet mass was fascinating, but the way Sage stirred the untouched flames within me was downright magical.

It was *real*. He felt it, too. *What could have happened?*

"Sorry about that. He's all clean now." Susan walks back into the room and deposits Zachary into the highchair next to the table. She scoops some veggies into a little plastic bowl then chops them up even finer before setting them in front of him.

I take my first spoonful of soup. *Delicious.* "You could be a chef, Susan. Have you ever thought about opening your own restaurant?"

She waves her hand in a dismissive manner. "I would never leave my farm." She rejects the idea immediately. "My father died a month after my twelfth birthday. A freak sailboat accident." Her expression bears the familiar lines of loss. Susan knows grief. "My mother never quite got over his loss. She held on, for me I'm sure, but she was never the same after he passed." Susan slowly brings her spoon to her mouth. After a long swallow, she rests it back in the bowl. "She passed herself, shortly after I met John."

The silence stretches between us. I need to say *something*. "How?" I finally croak.

"The doctor said it was due to heart problems. I think she died of a broken heart."

I drop my spoon in the bowl. The metal clangs against the stone, causing Zachary to startle. "Is there... is there such a thing?"

Susan shrugs. "There's no official diagnosis, of course, but I watched Mum lose her will to live. My dad was her everything."

The words ring too familiar for me. If I had never met Sage, if I had stayed focused on my grieving, I could have lost my own heart in the process.

Susan sips her soup. "John had dreams of big-city life. When I found out I was pregnant, he wanted me to sell my parents' land to finance a home in the city. I couldn't bear to leave their memories behind."

My soup grows cold. For the first time since Robbie died, I am talking to someone who truly understands. "Right. How could you just go on?"

"I grew up here. I loved this farm. I wanted Zachary to be able to run free in this paradise, rather than being imprisoned in the city." She watches him mash the veggies around on his tray.

"So Zachary's father left?" I hope it isn't too personal a question, but I need to know the rest of her story.

"He abandoned us to his dreams."

I wonder how much loss one person can survive. Robbie's death left me completely empty. I can't imagine another loss piled atop of that.

"I wanted to maintain a working farm, so we could remain here. After a long week at the computer, I figured out how to make that happen as a single mother," Susan says. "I couldn't control what happened to my parents or John, but I chose my destiny."

"Is that when you signed up as a WWOOFing host?" I refocus

the conversation on her, not ready even to think about what I want my destiny to look like.

"With a few helpers on the farm, I knew I could make it work." Susan rinses her empty dish in the sink, but her words radiate around me still.

I chose my own destiny.

I never even imagined I had a choice in the matter. My grief was just something that happened to me after Robbie died. The idea that I can take ownership over what happens next is powerful.

I *will* choose my own destiny. And it will not be a lifetime of sadness and crying but of possibilities, opportunities, and one day, maybe even new love.

Chapter 23

A s the sun begins to lower, I leave the comfy warmth of Susan's kitchen. She served coffee with her fruit crumble. For me, the best dessert was extra conversation.

The change within me is not a gradual subtlety. Instead, it looms and presses to be noticed. I'm finished with my self-isolation. I'm done wallowing in old grief. All because of Sage.

I carefully step down the gravel path to the dock. With each step, my resolve builds. First, I need to thank Sage for freeing me. He unwrapped the binds of loneliness and sorrow, and I will be forever grateful. But after my words of gratitude, I need to ask what happened to us. *That's* going to require a significant amount of bravery.

Sage sits on the weathered wood, running one finger back and forth over something in front of him.

"Hi," I say, quietly. Too quietly. After all of our embraces last weekend, the shyness has crept back so quickly.

Sage jumps up and joins me where the trail opens up to the water. "You came."

"Did you think I would stand you up?"

He shrugs. "I wasn't sure. I... I haven't been the nicest guy lately."

"Yeah, I noticed."

Regret flashes across his face.

"What happen—"

"Come and see what I've been working on." Sage takes my hand and leads me to the dock. When I'm sitting at the edge, he places a light object in my lap.

Thin strips of the lightest wood form a rectangular frame. A thin, transparent paper covers three sides, but the fourth features a familiar color and texture. I run my finger along the last purple envelope. "What is it?"

"The Japanese light these floating lanterns as a way to say goodbye to loved ones. They're supposed to guide spirits to their final resting spot." His fingers graze the purple envelope, careful not to touch mine. "You can even write a message."

Tears well in my eyes before trickling down my cheeks. Sage's thoughtfulness never ceases to surprise me. "You spent your entire evening building a lantern so I could say goodbye?"

He blushes then turns toward the water. The sun pauses along the waterline, causing the bay to glow with the oranges and pinks of sunset. "I would want somebody to do the same for me."

"Most guys would just be jealous of an ex."

He gazes toward the sunset. The colors illuminate his hair, and a glowing pink outline surrounds his body. He lifts his shoulders into a shrug. "Maybe that's what's wrong with the world. Nobody practices compassion anymore."

"Compassion?"

"As human beings, we should want to ease one another's suffering. We should put the needs of others before our own petty jealousies."

The golden light of the sinking sun shines around him, but I barely notice. Sage's heart is even more golden. "Is compassion what you meditate about every day?"

"One of the things." He finally faces me.

This is the moment. I've never initiated anything with a boy before, but the timing is *so* right. "I know how you can ease my suffering." I lean forward until my lips hover near his. He stares at me, not even blinking. When he begins to move back, I grab his hand. "Please," I whisper.

He takes a deep breath before glancing at me pensively. I brush my lips against his then meet his gaze once more. Sage softly presses his lips against mine. He traces the path to my ear with gentle kisses then whispers, "It wouldn't be right."

I cannot stop the tears that come with his rejection. "Wh—?" Before I can get a word out, he presses his finger to my lips.

He kisses each of the tears on my cheeks. "You've been through too much already."

His actions aren't matching up with his words. He's rejecting me, but he's also kissing me. I'm so confused. "What are you talking about?"

"I would be a burden." He finally returns to my lips. "And you've dealt with too many burdens already."

"Um, hello?" I glare at him. "Shouldn't I be able to decide my...?" The unspoken word—destiny—lingers, too personal to speak aloud.

"It's hard to make a decision if you don't know all the facts." Sage rubs one hand through his curls.

I've missed that familiar gesture. How have I become used to his quirks and mannerisms so quickly? I'm not ready to give him up. "What facts? What are you talking about?"

"I just meant that Robbie tricked you. He allowed you to fall for him before he shared all the stuff about his disease." Sage's voice breaks. "If you knew about his kidneys from the beginning, if you knew you would spend years of your life caring for him and then even longer missing him, would you have ever agreed to go out with him?"

He's blaming Robbie for not telling me. "Wh-what are you saying?"

"Was he worth it?" Sage whispers. "If you could go back and erase all your heartache, if you could be a normal college freshman, without all the sickness and death stuff, would you do it?"

No one has ever asked me this question. I think for a moment.

The idea of wiping away all of the bad stuff with one sweep of a wand is tempting, but it would wipe away all of the good memories too: cozying up under a warm blanket at Friday football games, dancing at Homecoming together, and hours of late-night phone calls. "He *was* worth it. I would never give up my memories to save myself pain. *Never.*"

Sage faces the water and raises his hand. His silhouette, dark against the setting sun, almost looks as though it's wiping away a tear.

How did this conversation get so heavy? I turn back to the lantern. "So I write a message on it?"

"You can if you want." He hands me a black permanent marker.

I think about what's left to say, but I said my goodbye in the cemetery. After months of pouring out my heart in never-to-be-read letters, I have nothing left to share. Slowly, I write out my final word to Robbie. Five last letters: *ADIEU*. Farewell.

"French?" Sage lifts one eyebrow.

"We took French class in high school. I used to tease Robbie about his terrible accent. He would come up with the most awful ways to say this one, until Madame Pompidou reminded him it sounded like 'achoo.'" I laugh at the memory. "That led to class-wide sneezing whenever we left her room."

Sage traces my upturned lips. "You don't seem as sad as when I first met you."

"Thanks to you," I whisper. "You helped me make peace with my memories."

He moves back abruptly then searches through his backpack until he finds a lighter. "Are you ready?"

When I indicate my readiness, he lights a small candle and places it on the bottom of the lantern. The candle's flickering glow illuminates the lantern in the now-dark sky.

"You should do the honors." He hands me the lantern.

"What do I do?" Soft lavender light pours through the last envelope.

"Place it in the water. Be gentle, though, so the candle doesn't go out."

I lie on my stomach then carefully place the lantern atop

the water. Small waves lap at it, and when I release my grasp, the lantern floats away on the current. Sage takes my hand and helps me up. We watch in silence as the lantern floats away, a tiny dot of light against the indigo water.

The last envelope is finally gone. I'm free to move on now.

Chapter
24

A small sliver of moonlight shines through the skylight, illuminating Sage's bed. I wanted to share so much during our silent hike back to the yurt, but I couldn't summon the courage. Instead of sleeping, I stare across the room at Sage's prone figure. While he lies in bed, his restlessness indicates he isn't sleeping any better than I am.

If Robbie taught me anything, it was that you can't risk wasting any time. Each moment is important. You need to make every one count.

I'm done wasting time. I'm finished with my inhibitions and cautiousness, both driven by fear.

I'm ready to live again.

I pull back my covers and climb out of bed. If I were to let myself think this through, I would slide right back into my cozy futon; instead, I step toward Sage's futon. With each step, the smooth wooden planks of the yurt floor remind me this isn't a dream.

As I approach, he turns over. His eyes widen when I step into the beam of moonlight, but he says nothing as I lay one finger across his lips then crawl in next to him.

"Abby? Wh—?" He begins to speak as soon as I move my hand, so I quickly replace my finger with my lips.

"Shh, no words." I kiss him again.

"But—"

"No memories of the past. No worries about the future. For tonight, let's just be in the moment." I gaze into Sage's eyes, trying to communicate how badly I need this. "Please."

For a long, silent moment, he stares back at me. Then he brushes his mouth along my neck, caressing each inch with tiny kisses. "In the moment?" he whispers against my ear.

I shiver as his warm breath caresses my skin then begin my own exploration. We lose ourselves in one another, until the moon lowers in the sky and the soft nighttime glow fades away.

I wake up in Sage's arms. Exactly where I want to be. He holds me tight, even in his sleep, and the skin-to-skin connection grounds me. *This* is living. Humans need this sort of togetherness.

I kiss the stubbly growth on his chin, which is quickly becoming one of my favorite parts of him. It's a reminder that I'm not a young teen, mooning over a smooth-cheeked boy. Instead, this is my first romance after the tentative steps into adulthood.

I need to approach things differently. Better communication is the first thing on my list.

Sage's eyes blink open, and he yawns. As soon as his lips close, I brush them with mine.

"What a way to wake up." He grins. "I had the most amazing dreams last night. There was this beautiful temptress who seduced me under the moonlight."

"Does her spell only work in the moonlight?" I run my thumb along the fragile skin between his neck and shoulder. "I wonder if it would work under the sunlight as well."

He scoots over until a space forms between us. "Abby, I—"

With the signs of more rejection coming, it's time to open up. "Can I try that radical honesty stuff again?"

"Are you trying to seduce me?" He props himself up on both elbows, only inches above me. "You are! First tempting me with being in the present, then your sexy talk about radical honesty."

I ignore his jokes and sit up, crossed-legged, on his bed. "For the first time in months, maybe even a year, I feel whole again. I don't want to isolate myself and hide away from others. Thanks to you."

"That was all you, Abby," he says seriously. "I didn't make you whole. You made those changes yourself."

"Before I met you, I was resolved to hide away with my grief. I could have done that for years or until the grief completely consumed me." I reach for his hand, and he doesn't pull away. "You challenged me. You reminded me that I could live again."

"But—"

"Let me finish." I stare right into Sage's eyes. "You helped me heal."

He gazes back at me. "You *have* changed. When you first came to the farm, you seemed broken. I'm *so* glad you've been able to rise above all that tragedy."

"I want to pursue whatever this is between us." I run one finger across the top of his hand. When he jerks slightly, I continue. "I know you feel the magic and the sparks just as much as I do."

"I do, Abby, but—"

"There's a reason you're pulling back," I whisper. "Tell me. Instead of shutting me out, tell me what's wrong. Please."

"I should." Sage won't even meet my eyes. "The whole time I've been at the farm, I've tried to pretend it doesn't exist. It's hard to start talking about something you've tucked away so deeply."

Sadly, I know exactly what he means. Sage and I aren't so different in the end.

Then it comes to me. His secret has to center on his future.

"Do you remember the day we watched the surfers?" I wait for his reaction. *Does he know where I'm heading?* "Remember how I won the favor and saved it for when I really need one?"

He slowly shakes his head.

"I'm calling in my favor, Sage." I scoot back until I'm at the edge of his futon. "I want to know what you're hiding from me."

Sage bites his lip. "I keep going back and forth between what would be easier—for you, not me. Should I tell you everything or protect you by sharing nothing?"

"I want to know."

"You deserve to know. I'm just afraid of making things worse in the end."

What could he tell me that would be that *bad? Why is he so worried about me?*

He grimaces and rubs his temple.

"Are you okay?" I place my hand over his, so both our fingers cover his temple.

"Yeah." He sighs. "Just a headache. They've been coming a lot this week."

"I wonder if Susan has some Tylenol?"

His eyes widen. "No, we don't need to bother her. I have some headache medicine."

"So, about your big secret?" I hate pushing him when he's not feeling well, but I'm so tired of not having answers.

"I'm thinking of the best way to tell you." Sage searches through his backpack until he finds a prescription bottle. He pops open the white top and pours a single pill from the orange vial. "Would you mind if I meditated on it, and we talked tonight?"

While I'm tempted to push him to spill his secrets immediately, his request's reasonable. Besides, it would be better to talk when both of us are at full capacity.

"Tonight?"

"Tonight. I promise." He brushes his lips against my cheek.

Chapter
25

We walk down to breakfast together. As we approach the covered table, the dining area sits empty. Stacks of pancakes rest upon two plates. Sage settles on one side of the table; instead of eating across from him, I sit next to him. His arm and leg brush against mine as he adjusts on the small bench.

I douse my pancakes in the fresh berries and whipping cream that Susan left then hand the containers to Sage. He waves them away and slowly slices a piece of pancake from his stack.

"Plain? What kind of health food kick is this?" I wrinkle my nose at him.

He slowly chews, still working on the first bite. "I'm not very hungry this morning."

"You're going to make me feel bad." I swallow another mouthful before continuing. "I can't resist Susan's cooking."

"No, I'm just… nauseous." He pushes his plate away then rubs his temple.

"Your headache's still bothering you?"

"Nothing I can't work through." He gets up, scrapes his plate, and heads toward the path. "I'm going to walk off this migraine. I'll meet you in the orchard in an hour."

Left to eat alone again, I take my time with breakfast. Susan had a carafe of coffee ready, and I pour a full mug of the steaming liquid. My volunteer time will be ending in two short weeks. At the very top of my list of things to miss will be Susan's home-cooked meals. The fast food crap served at my college could never compare.

Not that I'm welcome back there.

I've tried to stay busy so I don't have to think about what's next. When I return home, right after the holidays, my parents are going to wonder why I'm not returning to school. I can't hide it any longer. I'm done with all the deceit.

I'm finally strong enough to share how hard Robbie's death was on me. I'm ready to start something new.

I take my last sip of coffee then set off to find Sage. The path to the orchard passes right by Susan's house. She sits on her porch swing, rocking Zachary as he shrieks with laughter.

"Hey, little guy." I wave to him as I pass, then watch as he swings his hand to and fro.

"Hey!" he says. "Hey. Hey. Hey."

"Well, that's new. He learns something every single day, it seems." Susan watches him with an amused smile. "Heading to the orchard?"

"I'm going to collect the last of the fruit while Sage prunes the trees."

"Don't work too hard, Abby." She swings Zachary once again. "I've noticed you put in extra hours last week."

"No worries, I've enjoyed the work." I look past Susan's house to the view of the bay. "It's been… healing."

"I've always felt the same way about the old farm." She smiles. "My father used to say, 'A hard day's work is good for the soul.'"

"I can see why you chose to stay." I glance at the bay again. "I almost wish I didn't have to return home in two weeks."

"You're ready." Susan leans over the railing to pat my hand. "I can see the difference from when you arrived to now."

"Thanks." I stare at the leaves scattered along the trail, still uncomfortable with her compliments. "I'm going to look for Sage."

The path winds past the bay then curves into a small grove of trees. I step quietly into the orchard, watching for wallabies. They gather close to the entrance. When I enter into the hollow of the orchard, fruit trees surround me. The wallabies stand alert for a moment then hop to the opposite side of the grove.

I glance around for Sage. With the amount of time I took, he should have been here long ago. The stepladder's set up, the pruning shears lay on the ground, but Sage is nowhere to be seen.

The wallabies hop behind a cluster of cherry trees then scatter suddenly. I try to spot what startled them, but I only see a bit of blue peeking out of the grass. Not just any blue. Sage's blue shoe.

I run across the orchard. *Please be abandoned.*

My wishes are futile, though. The shoe's not abandoned. Instead, Sage's entire body lies prone in the grass, shaking uncontrollably.

"Susan!" I scream as loudly as I can, hoping she'll hear me, then fall to ground next to Sage. I place my hand on his shoulder, my trembles blending in with his body's violent shudders. "Help! Hurry!"

I cup my palm to the exposed side of Sage's face. "Sage, I'm here. Can you hear me?"

He doesn't respond. His body continues to shake.

Susan bursts into the grove. "Oh, no. He's seizing. Clear away anything he could hurt himself on."

She pulls out her cell phone. "We need an air ambulance immediately." Susan shares her location and other information, but I block out her words and turn back to Sage. He's still now, but nonresponsive. Sage, normally so vibrant and full of life, lies silently upon the ground.

"Please, please, please." My tears dot the cotton of his sky-blue T-shirt. "Sage, hang in there. Help is coming."

"He's stopped seizing." Still holding the phone to her ear, Susan whispers instructions to me. "Turn him on his side. Protect his head in case he has another one."

Another one?

Susan looks worried, but she's not panicking. She doesn't even seem that surprised. I mean, healthy guys don't just go falling on the ground with convulsions.

"Abby, Sage needs our help. Place him on his side." She mutters a few more things into the phone.

I place my hand against Sage's shoulder once again. His firm muscles contrast with the limpness of his arm. On his side. I can do this. I need to help him. I push against his shoulder while lifting at one of his belt loops. It works. He inches up to a sideways position. I position his arm and leg so he doesn't roll.

Susan's listening intently, phone to her ear. "Something soft? Yes. I have something right here."

Numbly, I take the soft bundle she hands me. Zachary's sling. Where is Zachary?

"Place it under his head," she directs.

I tuck the soft material under his head and neck then stroke his cheek. "Sage?" I whisper.

He doesn't answer. He doesn't move. The familiar cocktail of panic, fear, and despair return. Something is terribly wrong.

"Abby!" Susan's voice is sharp. She must have called me already, but it's so hard to do anything except stare at Sage's unmoving body.

"He *has* to be okay. I can't lose him, too."

Susan places her worn hands on my shoulders. She waits until I'm looking right into her eyes. "I need you to be strong. Zachary is alone at my house in his cot. He's probably pretty distressed by now."

All I can focus on is Sage. I try to pay attention to Susan's words. "Zachary?"

"I have to go to the hospital with Sage. I need you to get Zachary ready and meet us at Sydney Hospital." Susan touches my face then repeats her instructions. "I promised Sage's mother I'd be there if anything happened."

If anything happened? People knew something could happen?

"Go get Zachary. I'm calling the water taxi right now. Bob will meet you at the docks as soon as he can get out here." Susan pulls me to my feet then turns me in the direction of her house. "Pull it together, Abby. You need to stay strong."

Easier said than done. *How can I stay strong when I know the pain of losing someone?* She can't expect me to turn away from Sage when he lies unresponsive on the grass.

"Get Zachary!" Susan's sharp voice, so odd for her, forces me into motion.

As I stumble down the path, a loud whirring fills the air. I run toward it. A helicopter has just landed on the grassy clearing that overlooks the cliff.

"Which way is he?" calls a paramedic, jogging toward me with a large bag slung over his shoulder.

I point toward Susan and Sage then continue toward Susan's. *Get Zachary. Stay strong. Get Zachary. Stay strong.* The refrain plays over and over in my mind. But the words don't block the sharp pang of fear that radiates through my body. Sage was in terrible condition when I left him.

I left him.

If something happens... I left him in that field, just as I left Robbie when I went off to school. Even though he's not alone, I want to be the one who's there with him. I fall to Susan's doorstep as sobs overpower me.

Something's wrong with Sage. Susan knew. His mother knew.

Why didn't he tell me?

I don't think I can bear losing anyone again.

Chapter
26

Zachary's screams snap me out of my pity party. *Get Zachary. Stay strong.* I rush past the kitchen into the unexplored areas of Susan's home. A comfy sofa takes up most of the space in her modest living room. Zachary's screams resound down a narrow hallway. My footsteps echo off the wooden floorboards as I hurry toward his cries.

Zachary's door is open. He stands in his crib, grasping the railings with both hands. He shakes the wooden bars of his prison as he lets out another wail.

"Shh…" I reach into the crib and gently lift the little guy out. Zachary's face is bright red and tears streak his cheeks. He stops crying as soon as he is in my arms, but he continues to sniffle.

The sound of the helicopter lifting off spurs me into action. Zachary's already dressed, and I spot a stuffed diaper bag near the crib. Grabbing the bag, I head toward the door. "We're going to meet your mama at the hospital." I find some tissues and wipe Zachary's face while balancing him on my hip. By the time the buzz has disappeared, we're heading out the door.

Ten minutes later, I shift Zachary to my other side. I can understand why Susan relies on her sling so heavily. My right arm throbs from carrying him down the entire trail, but the pain barely registers. I'm *so* worried about Sage.

"Come on, missy," Bob calls. His motorboat bobs next to the dock, already secured. When I near it, he tosses me a tiny yellow lifejacket. "Susan's orders. Little Zac don't get anywhere near my boat without the jacket."

I fumble putting it on him, trying to support him with one hand while pushing and pulling the lifejacket on with the other. I end up with a tangled, screaming yellow bundle of baby. The urgency—we *must* get to Sage—only slows me down more.

"Hurrying ain't helping. Set him down on the dock so you have both hands." Bob smiles as if his directives have solved the problem.

Without a better idea, I rest Zachary on the dock. A ladybug crawls along one of the weathered wooden boards. Zachary stares at it, his crying ceasing immediately. As Zachary remains entranced by the bug, I untangle the jacket's harnesses and safely strap him in. He messes with the buckles that secure his chest, but they are seemingly baby-proof.

"Hand him over to me so you can climb in." Bob reaches out.

I grab Zachary, give him a little bounce when he begins to fuss, then hand him over. Holding the dock's rope railing in one hand and the motorboat's metal bar in the other, I step aboard. After taking a moment to get used to the small boat's constant motion, I sit in the most secure seat I can find, center of the boat, behind a plastic shield to protect us from the bay's spray.

"I'm ready." I nod toward Zachary.

Bob has been giving the baby the official tour of the small boat, along with a lesson on boat lingo. He pauses before handing Zachary over to me. "Well, living along the water, he'll need to know starboard, won't he?"

Bob's just being friendly, but I can't have a conversation right now. My focus remains entirely on Sage. "Please. Please hurry. I need to get to the hospital."

Bob revs the motor, and the small boat takes off across the bay, hitting the waves harder than I remember from my other crossings. I wrap my arms around Zachary, holding him as securely as I can. He doesn't seem disturbed by the bumps, though. Instead, he giggles with each bounce and lurch of the boat.

"Five o'clocker's leaving soon. You'll have to run to catch it." Bob pulls up to the town's dock. He helps me with Zachary as I climb off the boat. "Hurry!"

The diaper bag hits my behind rhythmically as I run, and my left hip aches under Zachary's weight. We reach the ferry's dock as they're withdrawing the landing ramp.

"Wait!" I wave a hand at the workers. "My friend was Life Flighted to the hospital. We don't have time to wait for the next ferry."

"Life Flighted? Is that an American thing?"

"I don't know what you call it here. A rescue helicopter came and took him," I say, as the ferry's horn blares.

Zachary reaches for my chest and grabs on. The worker's blatantly staring at my chest, but I ignore my embarrassment. "His mother's at the hospital, too. You can see he's kind of… hungry."

The ferry worker's cheeks blaze red. "Okay, but this is a one-time emergency exception. They'll have my job if I'm letting every pitiful story on the ferry late." He reverses direction with the ramp, so the metal once again connects the ferry to the dock.

"Thank you. Good deeds lead to good karma, you know." As soon as the words are out, I can picture Sage saying them.

"Wait until I secure it." At the sound of metal clicking, he waves me on. "Okay, hurry aboard. They're already radioing me about the delay."

"I can't thank you enough." I meet his eyes before hurrying up the ramp and onto the ferry.

Two frustrating hours later, I finally stumble into the lobby of Sydney Hospital. After the twenty-minute ferry ride, I found myself back in the confusion of Circular Quay. Sydney has many transportation options—ferry, train, bus, and even a monorail—but they all converge at Circular Quay. I studied the map for only a moment before Zachary began to wail. After bouncing him around and pointing out the boats on the harbor, he had calmed… until I glanced at the map again. I have no idea how Susan raises a child herself.

The only way I end up at the hospital is by the kindness of another mother who gives me detailed directions and a Ziploc bag full of goldfish crackers. I rush to the information desk. "I'm looking for Sage. Sage…" *How do I not know Sage's last name?* Real-world information—last names, phone numbers, addresses, and apparently, medical conditions—seemed so inconsequential on the farm.

"I'm going to need a bit more information, my dear." The matronly woman smiles at me patiently from across the desk.

"Um, the rescue helicopter. He was the one who arrived on the rescue helicopter." I gesture to Zachary as he begins to grumble once more. "His mother flew with Sage. The baby's really hungry, so I need to find her right away."

The women's eyes soften as she glances at Zachary. She turns her attention to the computer sitting in front of her. "Poor little guy. I should be able to find you a room number in the next few minutes."

I can't hold in my sigh any longer. Focusing on the baby's needs worked. Everyone wants to keep a baby safe, well fed, and happy. I'm eager to return Zachary to Susan so I can focus on my real urgency. Sage, convulsing on the ground, devoid of all awareness.

I blink away the tears that threaten to flow.

"Dear, don't cry. He's in room 207. Just take the elevator to the third floor then turn right." She wiggles her fingers at Zachary until he returns the gesture with a full-arm wave.

I hurry to the elevator, step side-to-side while waiting for the gleaming metal doors to open, and glance at the lit numbers as they make their slow progression from 15 to 0. When we finally board, I press the two with my shaking finger. Almost there. The question I couldn't let myself think of earlier comes rushing out. *Did I make it in time?*

The waiting room's sterile plastic chairs alternate between bright pastels: greens, yellows, and blues. Most of the chairs sit empty, but I spot Susan in a faded blue chair, facing away from us. She speaks rapidly into her phone, but I'm too far away to hear what the conversation's about.

Zachary holds out both arms. "Mmmumm. Mmmumm. Mmmumm."

"Zachary?" She spins around, phone still to her ear. "They just arrived. Thanks for everything." She turns the phone off before sticking it in her back pocket.

"Sorry it took us so long to get here. He wasn't very happy at times, so it took a while."

"Oh, baby." Susan rushes to take him. "You're probably starving."

In response, Zachary reaches toward her shirt.

Susan probably wants a detailed update of our trip into Sydney, but my sole focus is on Sage. "Is... is he okay?"

"When I left, he was resting in his room."

"What happened? Why did he have a seizure? How did you know what was wrong?" I can't staunch the flow of questions.

She leads me to a set of double doors, pulls the door open, and gestures down the hallway. "He's four rooms down on the right."

The corridor stinks of a nose-tingling antiseptic that stops me in my tracks. I know this smell. I spent far too many hours of my life breathing in this artificial odor. One sniff brings all the memories of Robbie back.

I *hate* hospitals.

I force myself to keep moving past the first three doorways, but I pause in the doorframe of the fourth. Sage rests against propped-up pillows in the narrow hospital bed. The green walls feature mounted paintings of ferns.

"Well, the good news is the accommodations are much nicer than at my hospital in Michigan." He smiles back at me. "The better news is you're my first real visitor."

"Your hospital in Michigan?" I take a step into the room. The surge of anger surprises me. I want to question him, find out every secret he has hidden from me. But relentless questions won't help.

They'll just spread my negativity around. "Are *you* okay? It was terrible. I found you. You wouldn't stop shaking. It was *terrible.*"

"I'm sorry you had to see that." Sage doesn't meet my eyes. "I'm sure it was traumatic, after..."

He doesn't need to finish. *After losing Robbie.* Even in this hospital bed, on the other side of the world, Sage thinks only of me.

"I should have warned you something like that could happen." He shakes his head. "I felt so healthy, I thought I was keeping it at bay."

Keeping what at bay? I cycle through the diseases I know about. *Epilepsy?* That's the disease that makes you have seizures, after all.

Before I can ask, a nurse enters the room. "Mr. Hansen, we have a few more tests to run. Are you ready?"

"See you soon?" Sage asks.

His voice sounds so hopeful, I can't help but answer, "Of course."

Chapter
27

The need to flee from the hospital stench overwhelms me. While Sage is poked and prodded, I find the elevator and escape to the main floor. *What kinds of tests are they doing? What could be wrong with strong, healthy Sage?*

A small café sits off to the side of the main lobby. Perfect. I order a peppermint mocha then sink into a soft armchair in the café's most isolated spot. The rich coffee aroma blends with the sharp, fresh scent of peppermint. I lower my face to the mug and inhale deeply.

Finally, the reminders of the hospital—of Robbie's last, terrible months—fade away. But my worries about Sage remain. People don't just fall on the ground shaking for no reason. Even worse, he *knew* something was wrong. But never told me.

I don't talk about my future. Sage's words haunt me. This must be why. The "something wrong" must be *so* terrible, so absolutely awful, that he can't allow himself to think of it.

I can't lose someone else I care about.

All day long, I held it together. I had to, for Zachary. But here, in this café, the tidal wave of emotion cannot contain itself any longer. Tears well then plop one by one into my coffee.

I *care* about him. After all these years of being so loyal to Robbie, I have finally let myself fall for someone else.

When I finally build up the nerve to return to his room, Sage sits upright in bed, supported by pillows. He smiles when he sees me reenter and waves me over to his bed. "I wasn't sure if you'd come back," he says. "Bad memories and all."

"I never told you how much I hated hospitals—"

"I guessed." Sage looks away for a moment. "I'm so sorry, Abby. I was hoping you'd never be in this position—here, in a hospital room, watching me grow sicker and sicker."

Sicker and sicker. His words confirm my suspicions. Something is terribly wrong with Sage. Silence fills the tiny, sterile room. Sage studies a tiny spot on the upper right wall, while I examine the linoleum floor.

"Is that why you avoided me for the last week?"

He scoots to the edge of his bed and pats the empty space next to him. I stare at it. All I want is to be wrapped in Sage's arms again. I cannot resist the temptation. I climb into the narrow bed, lay my head on his shoulder, and place my arm around his waist.

His lips brush against my hair; he holds me even closer and caresses my waist. For a moment, we enjoy the sanctuary of the present, avoiding any talk of past incidents or future worries.

"When you first showed up at Susan's, I figured you were escaping a bad breakup," Sage finally says. "Since you were always writing to Robbie, I assumed you were hoping to get back together when you went back home."

"I was so wrapped up in my grief, I never even wondered why you avoided the future."

"At first, it just seemed like a fun flirtation. But the more time we spent together, the more *real* my feelings became."

I lift my head slightly. *He had* feelings *for me?*

"When you broke down in the cemetery, it tore me up to see how much you were hurting. At first, I just wanted to make you feel better, but—" Sage studies the wall again.

"But?" I wish he would just reject me instead of drawing it out. It's torturous to wonder about all the reasons for his rebuff.

"I couldn't bear to hurt you all over again. I care about you too much to put you through all that."

He wasn't rejecting me due to lack of interest, but because he wanted to protect me. I lower my head back down to his shoulder, as his words really sink in. Whatever is wrong with Sage must be bad. Really bad. So bad, he thinks I'll end up losing him, too.

"What's wr—" I stop myself before I can ask. I'm not ready to know what's wrong. I'm not sure I can bear it.

"Abby, these weeks were really special to me." He leans down just enough to place a gentle kiss on my cheek. "I'm going to remember them."

"What if I'm not ready to say goodbye?" I finally find my voice. Sage may be sick with some mysterious illness, but I can still stand up for myself. "You did the impossible. You helped me to find closure, to *care* again."

"Care?" His voice cracks, gruff with emotion.

"You awakened something I thought was dead forever. I never believed I could care about someone again. I never imagined I could want anyone again." I raise myself up on one elbow, stroke the side of his face, and lower my lips to his. After a long, tender kiss, I snuggle against him once more.

He holds me close for a moment then moves away until he presses against the metal bed rail. "I promised myself I wouldn't be selfish. As much as I want to wrap you in my arms and never let go, it wouldn't be right."

His rejection isn't nearly so painful this time, because I can hear the regret in his words. "Because you're sick?"

"Really sick," he whispers.

"As much as I hate hospitals, I've forced myself to tolerate them in the past." I reach out until our fingertips touch. "I can do it again."

"I won't let you grow attached only to lose someone again." He sighs. "The more time we spend together, the harder it will be."

Lose somebody again. Lose *him*, he means. Sage thinks he's going to die. "It's that bad?"

"It's *that* bad."

I can't help thinking if we don't give a name to whatever's wrong, if we just go on as if it doesn't exist, it can't intrude on our lives. I weave my fingers between his and grip his hand. He freezes for a moment then draws me closer. We lie upon the thin, hospital-regulation pillow, so close our noses nearly touch. We stare into each other's eyes. I can't resist any longer. I bring my lips to his. I'm not going to leave him alone in this hospital. For tonight at least, I'll stay with him.

Chapter
28

"I told you this was a terrible idea!" The slamming door breaks the peace in the tiny room.

"Mom? You flew all the way here? How did you arrive so quickly?"

"I booked the first flight after Susan called," the woman's voice says.

My sleep-muddled brain processes the conversation as I struggle to fully wake. *Mom? Sage's mother's here?* As the metal rail presses into my back, I realize we are still in the hospital. I fell asleep next to Sage. I have sleep-infused memories of a nurse trying to force me to leave. Sage sweet-talked her into letting me stay, after sharing how he was all alone in a foreign country without any family to help him.

My eyes shoot open. I am cuddled up to Sage, in his hospital room, looking into his mother's curious gaze. Talk about first impressions.

I try to sit up, move off the bed, and run my fingers through my mussed hair at the same time. Sage grabs my hand before I fully descend. "Abby, meet my mother."

She nods at me before turning back to Sage. "You haven't taken this seriously since we've gotten the diagnosis. I said it the first time you made your plans, and I'm saying it again. Flying to the other side of the world instead of having surgery was foolish."

"When I have the surgery is my choice," Sage responds calmly. "I wasn't going to risk it without having lived a little."

I stand against the closest wall. This is a private conversation I probably shouldn't be hearing.

"So you pretend like everything's normal?" His mother shakes her head, unable to hide her look of disgust. "Farming, romancing girls, and all the while, the tumor's growing bigger."

Tumor? My breath catches.

"The doctor said it was slow-growing. She said I had time. She even agreed that it might be a good idea, given the... circumstances." Sage gives me a nervous glance. He hasn't forgotten I'm here, privy to this very personal conversation.

I edge toward the door.

"I know Dr. Ellington is a top-rated oncologist, but I never agreed with her decision." His mother gestures to the hospital bed. "Look at you, three months later, recovering from a major seizure. Who lets a tumor just grow in their brain? What's going to happen in three more months?"

The words circle around in my head. *Tumor. Oncologist. Brain.*

I flee the room. I was right. As soon as Sage's unnamed illness received a title, it became too real for me to handle. Cancer. The headaches, the seizure—it all begins to make sense. Sage has brain cancer.

His refusal to talk about the future makes sense, too. He must think he doesn't have one.

*W*hen I stumble back into the waiting room, I'm a mess. My nose runs, tears leak down my face, and my hands shake.

"Abby!" Susan rushes over to me and helps me to the nearest chair. "Are you okay?"

"Am *I* okay? Sage has freaking brain cancer, and you ask if *I'm* okay?" I hide my face in my hands and allow myself to sob.

Susan rubs my back with her callused hand while I cry. "You didn't know."

"He never said a word. All that talk about staying in the 'now' so he didn't have to say a word!" I pick up the closest magazine and chuck it across the room. My anger surprises me. When Robbie was ill, I never got angry. Don't get me wrong. A ton of other feelings inundated me; guilt that I was so healthy, and fear over losing him. Never anger, though.

"Zachary's been fussy cooped up inside." Susan touches my arm. "I was thinking of taking him for a walk around the city. Care to join me?"

"Okay." I need to escape this place. Hospitals are deceptive. Their shiny, sterile outsides hide their terrible truth; they are destroyers of dreams, wrecking person after person under the guise of help.

Susan leads me to the elevators, down to the ground floor, and through the maze of a lobby. I'm so numb, I barely notice a thing until we are out on Sydney's bustling streets. Hundreds of people crowd the sidewalks. Some stop to peer in the large glass windows of the stores that line the streets. Others walk in little groups, stopping often to chat with friends. A few move with purpose, quickly navigating their way through the crowds.

Sydney is filled with so much *life*. Exactly what I need.

"Thank you." I turn to her. "How did you know this would help?"

"When my mother died, I started catching the daily ferry to the city." She adjusts Zachary on her back when he starts to wiggle then continues walking. "I would walk miles every day through these streets. It was the only thing that helped."

Interesting how people choose to deal with their grief so differently. "I locked myself in my dorm room," I whisper. "After my boyfriend died."

Died. I can count on one hand the times I have used that word in relation to Robbie. *Does this mean I've started to heal?*

"Oh Abby, you've already lost somebody?" She places a warm hand on my shoulder.

So I tell her all about Robbie. Our love, our special purple envelopes, and *my* loss. It's only the second time I have made it through that story.

Chapter 29

"You have a big decision to make." Susan stirs her drink, a fruity summer smoothie.

"I know." I stare down at my latte, watching steam rise from the milky foam. "I don't know what to do."

"My dad used to tell me to trust my heart." She looks out the large window that brightens our table in the café. "I used his advice when John wanted me to sell the farm. I loved that place far too much to ever give it up."

"Do you ever miss your ex?" My biggest worry is that I'll make the wrong choice… and have to live with lifelong regrets.

Susan thinks for a long, drawn-out moment. "If you're asking if I made the right decision, I absolutely did. I never would have forgiven myself if I gave up the farm. Do I ever wonder what life would be like if I were married? Sure, who wouldn't?"

"I can't imagine walking away from Sage." When I think about listening to my heart's choice, the answer's clear.

"Do I hear a 'but' coming?" Susan turns to Zachary's highchair. She gives him another cracker.

"What if I can't go through all this again? What if I'm not strong enough? When I tried to be strong for Robbie, I nearly lost myself."

"So your brain's fighting your heart." Susan sighs. "Nobody can make this decision for you, Abby."

We sit in silence for several minutes, then Zachary begins to fuss. He tries to squirm out of the highchair's restraints and pounds his wooden rattle against the plastic tray. When he cannot free himself, he lets out a loud wail. Other patrons glare at Susan before turning back to their computers.

"One of my favorite things about this café is their private mum's room. A place to hang out with other mothers and their fussy babies. I'm going to change his nappy and allow him to toddle around for a few minutes."

I nod, happy to be alone with my thoughts.

My heart wants Sage. The thought of never seeing him again tears at me, but I'm so afraid to fully open up. The line between caring and love isn't so wide. I don't know if I can bear to love somebody again, knowing the whole while I am going to lose them.

I remember the patients from Robbie's hospital. The pediatrics floor housed the pediatric oncology patients, with their frail bodies and their telltale bald heads. I try to picture Sage with his muscle wasted away, his hair gone, and his strength non-existent.

Would he even want me to watch him sink one step closer to death with each new treatment he receives? Maybe it's better to leave with my memories of a happy, healthy, vibrant Sage.

But then he would be all alone.

My presence might give him something to fight for. Choosing to stay by Sage's side could be the one thing he looks forward to. He helped me come to peace with my past. It's only fitting I help him face his future.

Chapter
30

Susan and I sit side-by-side in the waiting room. Zachary plays next to us in a tiny area segmented off for children. He moves a large red bead along a wire then slides it back again.

"You can't avoid him forever." Susan pats my hand.

"I know." I have hidden away since we returned to the hospital. Walking into his room and declaring my intentions is such a big commitment. *Am I really ready?*

"Will you tell me what you know?" I need to be able to talk about this disease without breaking down before I face Sage.

"I don't know much, but I don't think Sage would mind me sharing. He emailed me a few months ago for the open volunteer spot. He never mentioned being ill or anything. Before he confirmed his place, his mother contacted me."

"His mother?" My cheeks blaze with the memory of my first impression. Choosing Sage would mean getting to know his mother very, very well. When children are ill, mothers often cope by smothering them with affection and attention. I remember Robbie's good-intentioned but interfering mother all too well.

"She shared that Sage was recently diagnosed with brain cancer. She also shared how he refused to have the recommended treatment right way. She spent nearly half an hour complaining about how he delayed his treatment for six months."

"He delayed his treatment?" His list. Sage must have been trying to get through his list.

Susan frowned. "It was almost like she was trying to scare me away from hosting him. In the end, I spent a lot of time reassuring his mother that we weren't in the outback, that medical care was a few minutes away, and that I would contact her in case of an emergency."

"What do you think the seizure means?" I have so many questions, and I've only asked the tiniest number of them.

"Abby, the doctors will know better than me." She pats me again. "You really need to be having this conversation with Sage."

Susan's right. I cannot delay seeing him any longer.

After the nurse buzzes me into the ward, I make tentative steps to Sage's doorway. I force a bright, cheery smile on my face before stepping into his room.

His sheets are still rumpled and turned down, but he's not in the bed. He's not anywhere in the room. I force myself to take a deep, calming breath before I look around. The little signs of Sage—a neatly folded pile of clothes, his shoes—are all absent. I take another breath. The spot for patient papers, located right outside the door, is also empty.

We've only been gone three hours. *What could have happened?*

I step closer to the bed and run my fingers over the cool metal railing. A few hours ago, I was cuddled up to Sage, next to this very rail. I breathe deeply again. I'm so close to panic these breaths are the only things that tether me.

I squeeze my eyes shut and run my fingers over the soft pillowcase we shared, until they snag on a sharp paper edge. I grab it and open my eyes. The postcard of Sydney's view from the ferry—the Opera House, the Harbour Bridge—sits upon the pillow.

When I turn the card, my gaze travels immediately to the signature. *Sage.*

I sigh and sink into the solitary chair in the room. Sage is okay. I'm not typically a worst-case scenario kind of girl, but my mind flung out all kinds of terrible situations. But he's well enough to write me a note.

Something is paper-clipped to the back, but I free it and set it aside. Tiny writing fills both sides of the postcard, lining every square inch of the rectangle. I read the first words:

Dear Abby,

I trace over those two words. How refreshing to receive a note rather than always being the one who writes them. It has been a long time since Robbie was well enough to send a note in the mail.

Lucky I had this postcard with me when I collapsed. I can think of no other way I want to share these words than on the back of one of our memories. Do you remember lining up the buildings on the ferry so the real-life scene matched my postcard? I particularly like that day's memories. It's when you first let go of your bindings, when I saw a true glimpse of the passionate, adventurous side of you. I really, really like that side. (See, I bet you enjoy my radical honesty!)

I am sorry. So sorry. I should have told you right from the beginning what I was dealing with. I don't blame you for running. I know this postcard might never even make it into your hands. I want you to remember our happy, sun-filled days at the farm. Cherish each memory. And most importantly, keep creating new memories.

Hugs and Kisses,

Sage

P.S. I really hope you get this postcard, because I left my most cherished belonging attached to it.

I unfold the thick paper to reveal a photograph of Sage and

me, kissing atop the Harbour Bridge. Its edges are tattered, and a thick crease mars its center, but the picture is a tangible memory of him. When I look at our embrace, I wonder how I ever doubted our passion.

On paper, our feelings are irrefutable.

How did Sage even get such a beautiful reminder of us? He hadn't left the farm since our trip to Sydney. On our weekend trip, we were together the entire time. Then I remember. Sage ran a quick errand while I was in the bathroom. He must have picked up the photograph snapped atop the bridge, but he never said a word to me. As I wipe blue denim fuzz off the front, the answer's clearer. He must have carried it around in his pocket.

The sweetness catches me off-guard. Sage may not be the conventional American guy; he's way too philosophical and alternative. But he's a thinker and a dreamer, and he has a heart of gold. The world would be a happier, better place if everyone walked around with Sage's eternal optimism and passion about living.

Did Sage really think I ran away? Away from his disease and away from him? I wish I could call him and tell him how I'm sitting at the edge of his hospital bed, waiting for him. But he's left no phone number, no address, no contact information whatsoever.

Sage doesn't want to be found.

Chapter
31

A nurse's aide rolls her cart into the room. She begins methodically stripping the bedding before she notices me still resting in the chair.

"Honey, what are you doing here?" she asks, holding his pillow in mid-air.

"I was looking for Sage." I'm not even sure how much time has passed since I found the postcard.

"The boy from this room?" She throws the sheets in her cart.

I nod. Words just seem too hard right now.

"His mama booked him an immediate flight home. She kept rambling on about how she needed to get him to a state-of-the-art facility in the States." The aide grins at me. "Like Australia's a third-world country."

"He's gone?" I had so much I wanted to say.

"They left not even an hour ago. I assume they're gone already." She places the last of the bedding in the cart then rolls it back to the doorway. "I've got to prep for another patient coming in. Best that you get moving."

"How is he? Will he keep having seizures? Did he recover from the one he had on the farm?"

"Honey, I gave you more information than I was even supposed to." She pushes the cart out of the room then turns back to me. "I hope you find the answers you're seeking."

I sit for another five minutes, staring at the picture of us. I love that there's proof of *us*. Sage couldn't have left me a better gift. I will cherish this memory we created together.

"Abby?" a familiar voice calls from the doorway. *His* familiar voice.

I turn toward Sage. He stands in the doorway, wearing a snug T-shirt and jeans. Without the hospital gown, Sage looks as healthy as can be. It's hard to imagine that only yesterday he lay on the ground convulsing. It's even harder to picture something so fatal growing in his brain.

"You came back," he whispers.

I stand up and throw my arms around him. I squeeze far tighter than I should, but my hug is more powerful than any words I could say. He wraps his arms around me, gently rubbing my back until my embrace softens.

I lower his cheek to my hair while I nuzzle in that comfortable space between his chin and shoulder. My hands run down his back, circle each arm, and pull his belt loops just a bit closer. I need to press myself against every inch of him, just to convince myself his return isn't a dream.

I lean back just enough to look at him. "I thought you left Australia."

His sigh ruffles my hair. "My mom's a panicker. She wanted to rush me onto the very next flight and spend hundreds of dollars shipping my things home, but we came to an unhappy compromise."

"Compromise?"

"I agreed to head home with her, after gathering my things and saying my goodbyes. Neither of us is very happy with the compromise."

"Is it safe? Are you allowed to be walking around like this?" I don't want him to harm himself because of me.

"Don't worry, the doctor cleared me." Sage gently squeezes my shoulder. "Listen, Abby. We need to talk."

Finally, I will have a chance to share everything with Sage. "I saw a little garden atrium when I was roaming the hospital yesterday. Can we go there?"

"Show me the way." He takes my hand.

I never want to let go.

I lead Sage to two full-glass doors that open into an indoor atrium. Tall, green plants grow under skylights. Flowers bloom from all manners of pots. A cobblestone path winds through the vegetation and leads to cast-iron benches, strategically placed for privacy.

We are the only ones in the atrium. Perfect.

"What a find, Abby." Sage twirls around. "Who would have imagined this could be hiding within the sterile walls of the hospital."

"It's like a refuge of life in a cesspool of d—" I clasp my hand to my mouth. I cannot believe that I came so close to saying the D-word to him. "I'm *so* sorry."

He guides me to the nearest bench, sits, and pulls me on his lap. He wraps his arms around me and whispers in my ear, "It's okay. You can talk about death with me."

"But you don't talk about your future."

"I didn't, until I traveled around the world. I met this brave girl who slew the dragons in her past. She showed me the secret to slaying my own dragons."

I shake my head. "I'm not brave. I run away from—"

"You *ran* away." Sage cups my chin with his calloused fingers. "Look how you're here, right now."

We gaze in each other's eyes. "Sage, how did you know I would come back?"

"I didn't, but I figured I better retrieve my most cherished object if you were gone forever. It would have been awful if that moment—the climax of our fairytale—was tossed in the garbage."

"I'm never going to be part of a fairytale." I turn away from him. *I'm destined to star in tragedies.*

"I haven't finished telling you my story." Sage traces patterns up and down my arms. It's hard to concentrate on words when his hands are so distracting. "So the brave girl conquered the dragon of her past and discovered the magical land of life. She went on to love often, live life heartily, and embrace every new experience. She found her happily ever after." He kisses me softly and tenderly on the cheek.

"What happened to the boy?" I force out.

"He returned to his own kingdom after having completed his quest. He climbed the highest mountain." Sage points to the postcard. "Kissed the prettiest girl in the far-away kingdom and lived life to the fullest."

"What if my happily ever after involves you?" I blink back the tears that threaten to fall. I promised myself I would stay strong for him.

His face falls. "I screwed up, Abby. I should have never done any of the 'now' nonsense."

"I've grown to love the 'now.'"

"Me too." He gently brings his lips to mine. "If only we were in a fairytale. I would find the magic amulet that could freeze time, stop the future from coming, and wipe away all memories of the past."

"That sounds lovely." I kiss him back.

He pulls away. "I feel like I deceived you."

"We both had secrets. We agreed it was okay to keep certain things private." I reach for his hand. "That's not deceit."

"But you still ended up hurt." His voice cracks.

Funny how hours ago, I was so angry with Sage for not telling me he was sick, but I can't bear to listen to his self-reprimands.

"We're dancing around the real issue." Sage stands up. "This is how I should have introduced myself. Hello, Abby. My name's Sage, and I have brain cancer."

Even after hearing his mother say the words and Susan confirming them, those two ugly words come to life when Sage utters them. *Brain cancer.*

I sit perfectly still and keep my face as expressionless as possible. "Tell me about it."

"My official diagnosis is low-grade astrocytoma. Astrocytoma. Doesn't that sound like a cool new star?"

Trust Sage to always put a positive twist on everything, even the name of his potential killer. "What does it really mean?"

He sighs. "I have a large tumor growing in my brain. Do you want the good news or the bad news first?"

How can he talk of good news? "Tell me the positive stuff." I can do this. I can have a conversation with Sage about his tumor without running away or sobbing or breaking down.

"So far, it's been a very slow-growing kind of cancer." Sage lifts me from his lap then stands. "That's why I was able to put off treatment for six months. My oncologist felt it wouldn't make a difference whether she operated that week or six months in the future."

I take Sage's hand and wander along the path. "Tell me about the bad stuff," I finally say.

He increases his pace. "According to my oncologist, the tumor's in an extremely risky spot to operate on."

"What could happen?" I don't want to know, but I need to ask.

"The bulk of the tumor is in my temporal lobe. That's the part of your body that controls hearing, language, and memory."

"So if they cut it out?" I can handle this. I *will* handle it, for Sage's sake.

He doesn't meet my eyes. "It's infiltrated actual brain tissue. When they remove the tumor, there's a chance I won't be the same afterward. Some people forget how to speak or lose their memories, but others might lose even more. I could end up with permanent brain damage, and that's if I'm lucky."

"If you're lucky?"

"Abby, many people don't even make it through the surgery." Sage studies me carefully. His eyes convey his concern. He's entirely focused on my reaction.

I try to swallow, but my throat's completely dry. Even though brain tumors can be fatal, hearing Sage list out all the potential outcomes makes it even harder to bear.

I *must* be strong. But I don't know if I can anymore.

"How can you stand here and calmly talk about your life ending?" I wipe away a stray tear. "Why aren't you screaming or crying? It's not fair!" I want to scream. I want to yell my frustration to whoever will hear it. *Why Sage? Why kind, sweet Sage?*

"I was having these reoccurring headaches—that's how I first was diagnosed—and when the doctor gave me the news, I realized I had two options." He sits cross-legged under a sunny window and pats the ground in front of him. "I could waste my time being angry, or I could spend it really living."

I sink down in front of him, cross my legs so our knees touch, and take his hands.

"My doctor scheduled my surgery for six months out. She gave me six short months. There was no way I was going to waste those months being angry at the world." Sage squeezes my hands. "I had six months to fulfill all my dreams."

"How are you doing on your list?"

Sage's face clouds. "Well, this seizure sort of messed things up. Mom already had the surgery moved up to next month, and I have to leave way earlier than I wanted to."

I release his hand so I can cup his face. "I'm going to be there for you, Sage. I am going to be with you every step of the way."

He brushes my hand away. "I'm sorry, Abby, but that's not what I want. I just wanted to say my goodbyes and head home... *alone.*"

Chapter 32

Sage doesn't want me. He would rather be all alone than have someone by his side. "Why? Why can't I help you through this?"

Sage remains in his crisscrossed pose. "Studying Buddhism has really helped me come to terms with my tumor."

"Can you tell me how?"

"Buddhist philosophy centers on suffering. Its causes, what helps, why humans suffer." He leans back and stretches his legs out until he lies in front of the window.

Maybe that's a sign this conversation will be too hard to have if we're looking at one another. I lie down, too, right by his side.

"The texts would say my tumor is not the cause of my suffering." He sighs. "Because death is an inevitable part of life."

"That's ridiculous. I mean, I know everyone dies eventually, but it doesn't seem fair for people to die before they've really lived." I can't help but think of Robbie. He never had the chance to go to college or move out of his parents' house or to celebrate his twenty-first birthday at a club. Life just isn't fair sometimes.

Sage rests on one elbow and looks at me with troubled eyes. I cannot believe how insensitive I've been. He's more aware than anyone of how much he might lose.

After a long, awkward pause, I ask, "So what is the real cause of suffering?"

"Attachment." Sage lies back down. "In my case, attachment to living, attachment to all those things on my list, attachment to..." He stares at me, wordlessly communicating something with his pointed look.

He couldn't mean he's growing attached to me, could he? I'm growing attached to him. Otherwise his rejection a few minutes ago wouldn't have been nearly so painful. Then the truth behind his words sinks in. Robbie's death would have never hurt so much if he were just another kid from my high school. My love—our connection—created the terrible pain and my unwillingness to let him go.

If Sage had introduced himself as the boy with brain cancer on day one, I never would have allowed myself to become so close to him. I would have been too scared to lose someone all over again. That's the flaw.

"Attachment may lead to more suffering." I lie on my side, facing Sage. "But how empty would life be without love? Without friendship?"

"That's exactly the argument I've been struggling with. I don't think the texts were saying never to get attached to anyone. I think they were saying be aware of how those attachments could be related to suffering."

"You love all this philosophy stuff."

"Well, I was a philosophy major." His eyes twinkle with excitement. "Radical honesty time. You're pretty cute when you're talking all philosophical."

"That's a turn-on?" He has to be kidding.

"Probably only for a philosophy major." Sage rests his hand on my hair. His fingers stroke my locks.

"Radical honesty time. I feel pretty attached to you."

"Oh, Abby." He runs his thumb along my hairline and over

my cheek until it rests at the corner of my mouth. "I can't fight my attachment, either."

I try to find words to respond but am distracted by the path his thumb took. Sage's lips—full and soft—are only an inch from mine. So tempting. Our lips meet. I show him my attachment through the slowest, softest, most tender kisses. When his tongue dances with mine, I know he's showing his.

He breaks away and gasps for air. "Spend tomorrow with me? It'll be my last day in Sydney."

How could I say no? Each moment with Sage has become precious.

Chapter 33

On the morning, I take the first ferry to Circular Quay. While waiting for Sage to show up, I head over to the street performers. The glass orb man performs, rolling his translucent ball along his body. As his actions increase in speed, the glass ball levitates in the air.

"Fantastic trick, even when watching it the second time." Sage embraces me in a giant bear hug. "I'm so glad we get to spend today together."

"Where's your mother?" She can't be happy I'm dragging her sick child around Sydney.

"I encouraged her to spend the day sight-seeing. I even left a list of the places she'd most enjoy."

"I sense a 'but' coming." I take Sage's hand. I don't want to miss one minute of contact with him.

"She'll probably stay in the hotel room on her computer, doing pointless research for the thousandth time." He sighs. "She keeps hoping she'll find a magic cure-all."

"You're her only son. Of course she'd want to do everything she can to help you." I understand standing on the sidelines, watching the one you love suffer. The fear of knowing it's only a matter of time until you lose your loved one forever.

"Besides, I don't want to spend my last day in Sydney talking about my mom." He leads me away from the docks. "Today's all about us."

"It's really your last day." He flies home tomorrow, but it still makes me sad to think of finishing my volunteer time without him. The next two weeks are going to be so lonely.

"We'll head to Susan's for dinner. She's fixing a special goodbye meal." He guides me over to one of the bus stops.

"What else do you have planned?" I glance at the bus destination. "The beaches? We're going back to the beaches?"

"I want to revisit some of our favorite spots on the hike." A city bus pulls up. Its brakes squeal as it rolls to a stop, and the doors open automatically. "Is that okay?"

I step aboard the bus instead of answering. While we did make some special memories at the beginning, I completely broke down mid-hike. *Why would Sage ever want to bring me back there?*

The morning passes without incident. Neither of us brought our suits, so we had to skip the inviting blue water, but we did make our way down to nearly every beach along our hike. At the last beach, Sage visits the refreshment shop and comes back with two double-decker ice cream cones. As I hike, I lick at the quickly melting cone, trying to catch each drip before it falls.

"Having fun?" He takes a big bite of his ice cream.

I'm not sure how to answer that question. I love spending time with him, but with each step we take, my dread builds. While I said my goodbyes to Robbie, I'm not sure I'm ready to face the cemetery again.

He picks up on my struggle and gives me the most awkward dripping-cone-in-hand hug ever. "There's a reason I wanted to come here."

"Yeah?" I nibble my cone and study the trail. Anything not to make eye contact right now.

"You've got a heart of gold, Abby." Sage places his free hand over my heart. Its beat intensifies under his gentle pressure.

"But putting everyone else first isn't always a good thing. You give and give and give until you have nothing left for yourself." He begins walking again.

The trail's rising higher and higher. We're nearly there. I wish we could just retreat down the trail, but he keeps moving. "Sage—"

He doesn't look back. "I know. You don't even want to see the cemetery."

So why is he making me do this? For a moment, his cold determination is so different from the kind-hearted, sweet Sage I know.

"We can't just pretend everything is fine." He takes my hand and walks around the next corner. Waverly Cemetery appears on the right side. "Abby, there's a fifty percent chance that I'll be lying in one of these next month."

The rows of gravestones, Sage's words, my memories of Robbie. It's all too much. I freeze. Sage glances at me, groans, and leads me to a small bench. We're not actually *in* the cemetery, but Sage makes sure we have a prime viewing spot from this bench.

"I know you want to come home with me," he says gently.

"I do. I want—"

"To take care of me," he finishes. "You're probably an expert at it, too. That's the thing. You're only nineteen years old. You *shouldn't* be an expert. You should be out living your life."

"I don't mind. I want to take care of you." I squeeze his hand. "Wouldn't it be easier to fight if I was right by your side?"

"It sounds tempting, but it would be selfish to ask you to sacrifice your life for a second time."

"Is it really a sacrifice if I'm doing it willingly?"

"What would make me happy is to see you actually enjoy life, create new experiences, make new friends, and see different places." He kisses me softly on my cheek. "Please, Abby. Since I'm not able to, would you be my eyes and ears?"

"I don't know." I couldn't go on enjoying life while Sage is in pain. It wouldn't be right. "What if I don't agree?"

He covers his face with his hands. I can barely hear his muffled response, "Then we say our goodbyes today and go our separate ways."

He would leave me? This living-life thing must be important to him, if he would end our budding relationship over it. I turn away from him and study the ocean.

"I just want to protect you from sacrificing yourself. If I don't make it, I need to know you won't lose yourself again."

"Who cares about all your attachment nonsense?" Tears roll down my face as I face him again. "There's this thing called grief. It's normal for people to grieve their loved ones when something happens."

Sage tugs at one of his curls. Even when he's frustrated, he's absolutely adorable. "Sure, grief is normal. We've all experienced grief. Locking yourself away from everyone, getting kicked out of school, running all the way around the world to get away, none of that is normal."

Touché. I don't even know to respond. I can't exactly deny any of his charges. I am guilty, guilty, guilty… of loving too much and too long and too deeply.

"If something happens to me, I need to know you'll be okay." His eyes plead with me.

"I can't promise," I whisper.

"But if you're in the habit of living, it will make it that much easier for you." Sage caresses my face. "It's going to be so hard to be bedridden for months. I want to see the world through your eyes."

I savor his gentle touch. Sage has seen me at my worst, guilt-ridden, lonely, and broken. He helped put the pieces together, after all. I can't blame him for wanting to protect me. Besides, he may be right. When my world revolved around Robbie, I had absolutely nothing left after he died.

Maybe practicing living will help, and if it makes Sage happy…

"Okay." I kiss his sun-reddened lips. "I'll be your eyes."

We spend the hour-long hike back to the bus arguing about the terms of our agreement. Our negotiations sound business-like, almost like they belong in a penthouse office suite rather than this beautiful cliff-side hike. Oceans, beaches with golden sands, the azure-blue sky, none of these have anything to do with negotiations or mediations.

"No daily letter writing," Sage orders.

"What's wrong with letter writing? I could be anywhere and still write letters to you."

"That's my entire point. You'd be more focused on making sure you wrote each day than on whatever else was going on."

He's so busy protecting me, he's forgetting to think about himself. About the joy each new letter brings, about the sense of connection and caring a hand-written letter provides. If Sage is going to think only of me, I need to focus entirely on him.

We pass a souvenir shop on the way to the bus stop, and the solution comes to me. "Postcards."

"What?" Sage looks into the store. "You want to buy postcards?"

"No, what if I sent postcards? I could only write to you on the back of a postcard." The idea makes me cringe a little. My thoughts and feelings naked on the back of the postcards for anyone to see.

Sage smiles. "I like it. You would have to keep visiting new places to get postcards."

"You'd truly be able to see the world through my eyes." I don't know if that's a good thing or not. He's right. I would need to make an effort to see new places. That's so far outside of my comfort zone I can't even imagine it.

"Okay, postcards." Sage beams now. "Our first compromise."

Chapter 34

The remainder of the long trip back to the farm continues in the same manner. We work out visitations on the forty-five minute bus ride. I refuse his "once a month" offer right from the beginning, and he rejects my "every single weekend" rebuttal immediately.

"If you spend every weekend with me, how will you be able to see new places? You're weekdays are already going to be super busy with school," Sage argues. School is one of his non-negotiable items. He wants me to enroll in my local community college so I can raise my GPA again. He insists an education is vital to being in the land of the living.

The bus rolls through the city streets. We're going to be back at Circular Quay soon, and I'm so tired of arguing about terms, I'm desperate to come to a compromise.

I sigh and throw up my hands. "Sundays. I can live life on Saturdays and tell you all about it on Sundays."

He smiles at me. "As long as you take the last weekend each month for bigger trips."

"Agreed." I don't have the energy to fight anymore. I can't figure out why this is so hard. I got over my fear of watching another person I care about die, but he's still not ready to welcome me into his healing.

Sometimes, thinking of others first has its downfalls.

After the doors open to our stop, we cross the street to the docks then watch as our ferry pulls up.

As we make our way up the ramp, he talks about therapy. Whether I should pick my own therapist, or he should try to find someone who specializes in bereavement counseling.

I walk to the railing, which overlooks the Opera House. When he joins me, still talking about options to help me get through my grief, I place my index finger to his lips. "Stop. I can't talk about this right now. We're passing some of the most beautiful sights in Sydney. I want to enjoy them instead of creating more terms."

He laughs. That wasn't the reaction I was expecting, so I turn to him.

"You want to live life," he says. "I got so trapped into planning for the future, but you remembered to live life." He kisses me above the backdrop of the Opera House. A slow, tender kiss that's full of his sweetness. I pull him closer until I am sandwiched between the metal railing and Sage's warm body. If only we could stay here forever.

This is our last ferry ride together. Tonight, he'll return to the city while I continue on at Susan's. I know only too well how this progresses. So I snuggle even closer, until every inch of my body presses against his. We savor one another as our ferry makes its way along the harbor.

The water taxi finally arrives at Susan's dock. Sage steps off then offers me a hand. We hike hand-in-hand to Susan's house. I don't ever want to let him go.

I'm forced to, though, when Susan runs out her kitchen door, heading with open arms for Sage. She embraces him so hard, I'm worried he'll pop.

"You absolutely terrified me," she scolds him. "When I heard

Abby screaming, then saw your limp body in the grass..."

I shudder. I had the same reaction.

"I'm sorry about that. I never thought I could actually have a seizure." He runs his fingers through his curls. "I mean, the doctor mentioned seizures as a possible symptom, but I never imagined—"

"Now don't get all guilty before our party." Susan pats his shoulder. "I'm just glad we have the opportunity to say our goodbyes."

Her words have a double-edged meaning, as if she means our permanent goodbyes. I've never thought of Susan as fatalistic. Maybe it's not fatalistic, though. She always has been a realist, and she's facing the situation—more bravely than I did—with the information she's been given. In spite of Sage's endless optimism, he too considers the worst-case scenario endings.

Maybe I'm the only one who still believes Sage will survive. I have to believe he will. If I don't, I have no hope left to cling to. And I never want to be hopeless again.

"I'm still preparing our meal," Susan says. "I'll need about an hour to have it all ready."

"Perfect. I'm going to pack up my stuff, then I want to take one last walk around."

One *last* walk. No talk about returning to the farm one day instead of acting as if it's the final hike. I need to distract myself before I lose myself in the spreading waves of grief.

"Do you want company on your walk?" I ask.

Sage considers my offer. "I think I'm going to need some privacy. Do you mind if I go solo?"

I'm relieved, actually. I need to take a break from all the intensity. I need time to regroup and gather my strength.

"I could use some help in the kitchen. Would you mind, Abby?" Susan looks toward her open doorway. "Things are going to burn if I keep chatting out here."

"I'll be right in." Talking with Susan will be the perfect way to figure out how I'm really feeling. She's become a good friend without me even realizing it.

That's when I realize just how much I've recovered from losing

Robbie. I want to seek out the comfort of a friend, rather than lock myself in a room all alone—that's healing. If I can heal from Robbie's loss, I can handle anything Sage throws my way. I'm ready, brain cancer. You're not going to break me.

Chapter 35

When I step inside Susan's kitchen, the aromas wafting off her stove tempt me. A yellowish sauce, speckled with red, bubbles in a pan on the back burner. Rice noodles soak in another pan. An empty wok sits on the largest burner, while her rice cooker steams away.

"I thought I would make a Thai feast for Sage." Susan hurries from pot to pot, stirring and sniffing each one. "I know how fond he is of all that Asian stuff."

"It's perfect." I spot colorful paper lanterns and intricately designed silken tablecloths piled up. "He'll love it."

"I hope so. Cooking is my way of coping, you know." She adds chopped pumpkin to the yellow sauce then throws in a handful of cut-up potatoes. "I pour all of my feelings into the food."

"Does it help?" I'm still gathering my coping strategies. On the surface, this frenzied, manic cooking seems to calm her.

"A little. When I think about his age, though—" She throws a pile of tofu into the spluttering oil at the bottom of the wok. "He's not much younger than I am. If something happened to me, who would be there for Zachary?"

That's the thing about death. It makes people reflect on all the worst-case scenarios out there. I try to bring Susan back to the present. "How old are you?"

"Twenty-nine."

"Twenty-nine? Really?" I would have pegged Susan to be in her mid-thirties. She has a maturity about her, so different from that of the people I went to school with. But she's experienced loss, too. Maybe grief ages people.

"I know I look older than that. It's hard to retain your looks when you have the stress of a farm and a baby and..." She wipes a tear away. "It has been a long time since I've had a good friend. Sage reminds me of my friends' brothers, joking, silly, and playful. I guess I've grown a little attached."

"Attached." I sigh. "Please don't use that word with him."

"Why?" She turns away from the pots and the pans. "What happened when you returned to the hospital?"

It's been a long time since I've had a good friend as well. Susan's support, understanding, and willingness to listen help me open up. I share everything. His empty bed, the postcard, his reluctance to continue our relationship. We talk about all the rules he's constructing for us going forward.

"Sounds like he's more afraid than you are," she notes.

"Afraid?" I get why Sage would be afraid of dying, but not why he would be afraid to accept love from those around him.

The buzz of the rice cooker interrupts our conversation. Susan jumps up then simultaneously stirs two pots before they burn. "The food's nearly ready." She points to the pile of lanterns and silks. "Can you decorate the outside while I make the finishing touches on our meal?"

A few minutes later, the paper lanterns flicker with candlelight atop Asian-inspired tablecloths. Tonight's food covers one table, while the other is set with Susan's best dishes.

"Let's call our friend." She reaches up and rings the dinner bell.

age hikes down the path a few minutes later. "I'm going to miss that bell." He pauses while he takes in the twinkling overhead lights, the flickering lanterns, and the buffet of food.

"Welcome to your Thai feast." I wrap my arm around his waist. Our minutes are dwindling away.

"Pumpkin curry, pad Thai, and a mango-cashew stir fry. All vegetarian, of course," Susan says.

"You didn't have to go through all this trouble. I would have been happy with PB&J." Sage embraces Susan in a big hug. "Thank you, though."

"You'll appreciate it more after a few days of hospital food. I don't know how it is in the States, but the food's barely edible in our hospitals."

For a moment, nobody speaks. The uncomfortable reminder of what Sage faces lingers in the air.

"Thanks for being able to talk about it." Sage takes his plate and piles it high with food. "Too many people are afraid to even mention I'm sick."

"They don't teach social niceties for disease and death." Susan scoops curry onto her plate. "Since I'm being blunt, what did the doctors find?"

Sage sets his plate on the table and slowly lowers himself to his seat. "The tumor actually grew a little bigger over the last few months. It wasn't supposed to do that."

Things freeze. *The tumor was growing?* I'm no oncologist, but even I know that's not a good thing.

"See, another one of those things you think you can control," Susan says. "Nobody can stop a tumor from growing. That's its whole life purpose."

"What do you mean, *another* thing I can control?" Sage hasn't eaten anything.

"Abby told me about all of your negotiations."

He stares at me. I glare at Susan.

Susan just shrugs. "It needs to be talked about. I'm not afraid to play the bad guy when I'm really being a good friend to you both by being honest."

"I'm not going to let Abby get hurt." Sage studies his plate.

"You really think you can prevent her from getting hurt?" Susan places her hand on Sage's. "If the worst happens... I hope it doesn't, but if the worst happens, Abby is going to be devastated. If she wasn't devastated, she wouldn't be worth keeping around."

Sage glances at me, but now I'm busy examining my plate. Susan's right. If something happens to Sage, I will be devastated. I won't tell him that, though. If I thought his stipulations were annoying now, I can't even imagine how restrictive they will become.

"If you die," Susan says. "I will grieve for you. I will cry, and I will curse the skies, and I may even throw things."

I wonder how she keeps her voice so calm when talking about all of this.

"No, I don't want anyone crying for me." Sage pushes away his uneaten plate of food then gets up from the table.

"But we will." Susan reaches for his hand. "Because we care for you. You cannot control the grieving process of others any more than you can control that tumor growing inside of you."

"I can't handle hurting anyone!" he yells.

"You're not hurting anyone. That unnatural thing inside of you deserves all the blame." Susan rises, still grasping his hand. "You've become a dear friend. Without your help, I wouldn't have been able to keep this old farm running."

"Susan—"

"Let me cry for you." Susan begins to cry before pulling him into a final hug. "Goodbye, Sage."

Sage shakes off her embrace and breaks into a run, his untouched plate still on the table.

Susan grabs my arm before I'm able to follow him. "Give him a few minutes. He's down at the docks, and he probably needs some alone time."

"Why would you do that? Why would you ruin his last night?"

She stares quietly at the dark path to the docks. "I've experienced enough loss to know that nothing good comes from deceiving yourself."

Chapter
36

Sage sits on the wooden dock, staring out at the water. In the distance, the lights from the nearby town reflect off the water's surface, providing the only luminosity in tonight's moonless sky.

He holds one of the paper lanterns in his hands. It's still lit, and the candle's soft glow illuminates his face. I sit down next to him, and we both gaze into the candle's flame.

Several minutes pass in complete silence. "How are you?" I finally ask.

"Saying goodbye is so much harder than I thought." He sighs. "And I'm going to have to repeat the whole darn thing with my friends back home."

"Did you think it would be easy?" I take his hand. *What was he expecting?*

"I didn't think." He shakes my hand away. "I just shut out all thoughts about the tumor and the surgery and all the terrible outcomes."

I remember being in the same place. Not wanting anyone to mention Robbie or prepare me for his almost certain death. I wouldn't talk to my parents, my friends, or even the social worker in the hospital. The conversations would have been that much harder if they were about me instead of my boyfriend.

"I thought if I became skilled enough at this Buddhism stuff, I could just handle… anything." He laughs but not his normal, happy sound. "I really believed when I left here and *had* to deal with it, I would be able to just accept my path."

"Sage, you have the right to be angry and sad and afraid." I wrap my arms around him and lower my head to his back. "That doesn't mean you failed anything. It means you're human."

"I don't want to hurt anyone." He continues to face the water but leans back into my embrace. "I don't want to cause you more pain, I don't want to leave my mom all alone, and I don't want to make anyone sad."

"But don't you get it? You wouldn't be hurting and abandoning people, the cancer would." I kiss his temple.

"Do you want to know what's worst of all?" he whispers.

"Tell me." My lips still rest against his temple.

"I feel so selfish, because a part of me wants to focus entirely on what I'm going to be losing." His shoulders begin to tremble. "I want to travel more—visit all seven continents. I want to finish school. I want so much more." His tears fall onto my arms. I hold him even closer. "I don't want to die," he cries. "I'm not ready. I've tried to prepare myself, but I'm just not ready."

"What twenty-one year old would be ready?" I kiss away a tear that slides down his cheek. "Wanting to live is normal."

He flips around so I'm still holding him, but we're face to face. Sage gently lifts me into his lap, holds me close, and continues to cry softly against my shoulder.

For the longest time, I comfort him in the only ways I can. A gentle embrace, open ears, and caring words. "Do you know what really helped when I was lost in my grief for Robbie?" I finally say. "Talking about him. When I kept my past all shut off, it started to overtake me."

Sage doesn't respond, but his crying softens.

"You've never talked about your future. Maybe it would help if you shared your dreams."

"I don't know. What if putting it on the table makes everything worse?"

"Can it get much worse from how you're feeling?"

Sage readjusts me until I'm sitting between his legs, staring at the water. "There's this graduate school I really want to attend." He wraps his arms around my waist, holding me close to his solid chest. "It combines western psychology with eastern practices."

"You want to become a meditating psychologist?" I can't help but giggle.

"I just think combining the two could help more people. The school's in the mountains. I'm done with Michigan. I want to spend some time in every habitat."

"So the mountains for graduate school and…"

His soft breath tickles my hair. "Maybe an area with beautiful old-growth forests when I begin my practice."

"That sounds nice." I try to picture myself in his dream. I wouldn't mind escaping from boring old Ohio.

"Travel. I forgot to mention how much I would travel. Each vacation, I would go somewhere new." He kisses me on one cheek. "Hopefully, with a pretty girl by my side."

Maybe he has inserted me into some of his dreams. I know he has become a part of mine.

"Sometimes the trips will be for fun, but I'd like to do some volunteer trips, too. Maybe digging wells in a village without clean water, or helping to build houses after a natural disaster." He sighs. "I want to help people. Make the world a better place."

This is why I love Sage. Even when faced with a potentially fatal disease, he never stops thinking of others.

Love. For the first time, I realize how deeply my feelings have grown for him. With Robbie, my feelings developed slowly, over the course of several years. I never would have thought it possible to have such intense feelings for a boy I met just a few weeks ago.

Only we didn't meet under normal circumstances. Instead of an occasional date or a single class together, we spent nearly every waking minute together. Rather than casual flirting and fun, a whirlwind of feelings threw us together.

When you face death, and when you have experienced death's

aftermath, time moves differently. Each moment becomes more valuable, more precious, and more meaningful. Sage and I may have spent only three weeks together on Susan's farm, but it probably was the equivalent of three years of dating, given what we've been through.

I love Sage. I test out the idea in my mind. I'm surprised to find that my heart soars, and I don't feel the tiniest bit of guilt. I really love Sage.

It's different from my feelings for Robbie. When Robbie and I were young teens, the excitement of first love and the awkwardness found only in teen love filled our relationship. These feelings toward Sage may be a more grown-up version of love. I want to protect him, and he's shown that he'll be self-sacrificing to protect me. I might lose him, but the idea of never having met Sage is worse than the thought of losing him.

What's that old saying? It's better to have loved and lost than never to have loved at all.

That old poet was right. I'm a better person for having cared for Robbie so deeply, and Sage continues to help me grow each and every day.

"And when I've traveled all around the world—" Sage holds me even snugger. "I want to marry the love of my life and start a family."

Has he been thinking about love, too?

"Thanks, Abby." He slides me forward until my head rests in his lap. Then he leans forward and kisses me, completely upside down. "It really helped to think about my dreams again."

"You can't look at the percentages and let that determine your outcome." I sit up and face him. "You need to go into this surgery thinking, 'I will survive.'"

"Are you saying I should let go of my pacifist ways and become a fighter?" He smiles.

"Exactly. You need to need to fight with every bit of energy you can summon up." I look into his eyes, so dark out here in this moonless sky.

He puffs up his body and shows his muscles. "I will throw down that bloody cancer on its skinny little arse."

"Three weeks later and your Australian accent hasn't gotten any better." I laugh. "It sounds like you're repeating bad British comedies rather than words from the outback."

A light shines in the distance, heading our way. "My water taxi will be here any minute."

"I thought they didn't come this late at night." While he said he was leaving, I had hoped we might be able to have one more night together.

"Not normally, but Susan made special arrangements... given the circumstances." He makes a face. "I never wanted to be one of those people who got special treatment due to their problems."

"I'm not ready to say goodbye." A few tears slide down my cheek. I blink back the others and force myself to calm down.

"My flight leaves at dawn. I need to go."

"I know."

Do I tell him? Do I share those three words with him before he goes? I'm not sure if they would help him—give him something more to fight for—or stress him out. I don't want him to spend the next few weeks worrying about me.

Knowing how Sage always puts others first, it would probably be the second. He would fret and worry over those words meant to give him comfort. So I hug him, kiss him, and whisper other sweet words to him.

I help him gather his things. The boat pulls up, a single light in the darkness of the water. I hand each item to him on the boat. I pull him across the watery gap for one last hug and a long, long kiss. Only when he has sailed away into the night do I whisper my three words onto the water.

I love you.

I love you, Sage.

I hope more than anything that I will have the opportunity to speak those words face-to-face one day. For now, I lose myself in my tears. No one can be strong forever.

Look for the second book in the Wander series in late 2014.

If you would like to continue Abby and Sage's journey, please sign up for my newsletter. It's the best way to learn about my new releases. Newsletter members will also be given opportunities to participate in special giveaways and sales.

Anna's Updates: http://eepurl.com/R9OfT

Other ways to stay connected:

My website: http://www.annakyss.com/
Facebook: https://www.facebook.com/pages/Anna-Kyss-Author
Twitter: @AnnaKyss
Email: annakyss@gmail.com

Acknowledgments

I am lucky enough to have a real-life Susan in my life. My sister always has yummy food in her kitchen and an adorable baby on her hip. Jenny, you were the inspiration for Susan. It's only fitting since most of the novel was written on your upstairs couch.

Other books by Anna Kyss

PARANORMAL ROMANCE

Wings of Shadow (The Underground Trilogy, Book 1)

Wings of Memory (The Underground Trilogy, Book 2)

DYSTOPIA

Cerulean